A Problem in Prague

By Noah Webster

A PROBLEM IN PRAGUE
AN INCIDENT IN ICELAND
A PAY-OFF IN SWITZERLAND
A WITCHDANCE IN BAVARIA
A BURIAL IN PORTUGAL
A KILLING IN MALTA
FLICKERING DEATH

A Problem in Prague

NOAH WEBSTER, pseud.

PUBLISHED FOR THE CRIME CLUB BY
DOUBLEDAY & COMPANY, INC.
GARDEN CITY, NEW YORK
1982

All of the characters in this book
are fictitious, and any resemblance
to actual persons, living or dead,
is purely coincidental.

Library of Congress Cataloging in Publication Data

Webster, Noah, 1928–
A problem in Prague.

I. Title.
PR6061.N6P7   1982   823'.914
AACR2
ISBN 0-385-17944-8
Library of Congress Catalog Card Number 81–43398

First Edition in the United States of America

For Craig.

Queen's and Lord Treasurer's Remembrancer.
H.M. Exchequer Office.

para. 28. "also deals with the collection of Income Tax for certain Government Departments. In practice, the Departments transfer monthly to the Income Tax suspense account of the Queen's and Lord Treasurer's Remembrancer as banker the total tax collected."

A Problem in Prague

CHAPTER 1

It was going to be a reasonable day, or it looked that way.

Edinburgh had wakened to a sunlit morning. The sky was clear, the last few traces of overnight mist had almost faded from the grey roof-tops of the Scottish capital. High above Princes Street's rush-hour traffic, the view from Edinburgh Castle stretched for miles over several counties.

At least it wouldn't rain.

In Leith Walk, a drunk was booted out of a doorway where he'd spent the night. In Lothian Road, two teenagers with toy guns and a very real butcher's knife were robbing a Post Office. In their Princes Street hotel room, a honeymoon couple from Canada had begun their first real quarrel. At Waverley Station, a distinguished churchman about to board a train was ten seconds away from a coronary attack.

Jonathan Gaunt ambled through Princes Street Gardens, hands stuffed into the pockets of his grubby sheepskin jacket, on his way to work and reasonably content. Though the Gardens were in the heart of the city, the growl of traffic was far enough away to be incidental. He could hear birds singing, the trees showed a start of new greenery, and the first spring daffodils had begun to flower.

Two girls, the only other people in sight, had stopped a little way ahead. They wore denim trousers, heavy wool sweaters, and walking boots. One had short blond hair and was taking a photograph of the Scots-American War Memorial. The other had long dark hair, good looks, and was carrying a shoulder bag which had a small Danish flag sewn to the front flap.

Gaunt stopped, waited until the camera shutter had clicked, then walked on. As he passed, the girl with the shoulder bag murmured her thanks.

He winked at her. She smiled then watched thoughtfully as

Gaunt started up the steps which led to Princes Street. Men like that one, she decided, could set more than her imagination going. But no woman—no Danish woman at least—would have allowed him out with a sheepskin like that, the seam of one shoulder burst and gaping open.

He vanished from her sight. She turned back to her friend.

Edinburgh's Princes Street is department stores, shopping crowds, and the occasional parade. George Street, running parallel behind it, is a prestige business address with Victorian buildings trying to look Georgian while they frown out at some of the worst parking chaos in Western Europe.

The usual fighting patrols of blue-uniformed traffic wardens were slapping parking tickets on cars as Gaunt walked along. The sight brought a twinkle to his grey-green eyes.

He was a tall man, compact in build, in his early thirties, with unruly fair hair and raw-boned features. Under the sheepskin jacket he wore a light-weight tweed sports suit with a faded blue shirt and a knitted tie in a darker blue. His mocassin-style shoes had taken their share of wear.

Particularly in the last couple of weeks, since he'd sold his car and transport had become a matter of city buses and his own two feet. But at least pedestrians didn't get parking tickets.

Temporarily, though not for the first time, Jonathan Gaunt had a cash-flow problem. He couldn't go near his bank overdraft until the next pay-cheque.

Disaster had struck from the world of stocks and shares, his normal pocket money playground. A small construction firm which should have blossomed overnight had gone spectacularly bankrupt, the company secretary's last known address being c/o South America.

Gaunt shook his head at the memory. The nearest traffic warden, a woman with a face like a blunt axe, glared as he walked past and went in through the doors of the Exchequer Office.

It was a large building, home for several Civil Service departments. Gaunt worked for the Queen's and Lord Treasurer's Remembrancer, located two floors up. As he crossed the lobby towards the broad stairway a uniformed attendant intercepted him.

"Looking for new wheels yet, Mr. Gaunt?" asked the man.

"Soon," said Gaunt. "I'm thinking about it."

"Right." The attendant was elderly, sporting a double row of medal ribbons from World War Two. He lowered his voice. "I've a brother-in-law in the used-car game. Crooked, but he owes me. So . . ."

"I'll let you know," promised Gaunt.

He climbed the stairs to the Remembrancer's Department, went through the modest main office where covers were still coming off typewriters, and reached his room. It wasn't much more than a cubby-hole with a desk, a chair, and a filing cabinet. But as an external auditor he wasn't there often enough to need more.

Getting out of the sheepskin, tossing it on the cabinet, Gaunt slumped into his chair and yawned. Maybe thirty-four-year-old civil servants weren't supposed to be up at 3 A.M. taking pain-killer tablets. Not too many of them drew army disability pensions for a broken back that would never totally heal.

He eyed his desk moodily. There were two case files on it, neither of them urgent. It might be an idea to call John Milton, his stockbroker and once-a-week poker partner. Milton was cautious enough to regard a hand with four queens as a risky gamble. Even Milton had raised only mild objections to his buying the Cayward shares on a play-the-margins basis.

Except there were no margins left when a firm collapsed.

Gaunt started to reach for the telephone. It rang instead and he looked at it in surprise, swore as it kept on, and finally answered.

"Jonny?" The woman's voice at the other end didn't pause. "He wants you. Come through, will you?"

The line went dead. Gaunt replaced the receiver, rose, and went out into the main office. He saw the office junior spooning instant coffee into mugs.

"Leave mine," he told her. "Maybe later."

A summons from Henry Falconer, senior administrative assistant to the Remembrancer, couldn't be ignored at any time. But it amounted to a command when it came through his secretary. Her name was Hannah, and Gaunt knew from bitter experience that any time she called him "Jonny" there was trouble ahead.

Hannah was at her desk when he went into Falconer's outer office. A well-built brunette, she looked up from a notebook she was studying and gave him a suitably distant smile.

"You'll have to wait." There was annoyance behind the words. "He's on the telephone—his wife called a moment ago."

"That won't improve his mood." He had a brief, fantasy vision of Falconer's wife wearing jackboots and cracking a whip. He'd only met her twice, but she qualified. "How about you Hannah? Still visiting that friend in hospital?"

"Yes." She hesitated, with the beginning of a flush. "Why?"

"I wondered how she was," said Gaunt.

One day a week, every week, Hannah took a considerably extended lunch-hour to make the alleged hospital visit. Almost always, Henry Falconer performed a similar vanishing act after making noises about a meeting he had to attend. Whatever went on, whether they ever did more than hold hands at a lunch table somewhere, Gaunt reckoned it was none of his business. But he wouldn't have told Hannah that.

"My friend is still ill," Hannah said defensively. "Any time I take off, I make up."

"I'm sure Henry appreciates that," said Gaunt.

Her face froze and she turned back to her notebook.

There was a framed photograph of Queen Elizabeth on the opposite wall, Government issue. With nothing better to do, Gaunt eyed the soft-focus picture with humour. Elizabeth the Second of England had to change her title to Elizabeth the First of Scotland the moment she stepped over the border. At the start of her reign, enthusiastic Scottish nationalists had either howled in protest or planted bombs if an E.II R cypher appeared.

Scotland was stubbornly sensitive about her national status within the United Kingdom. It was one of the reasons why the archaic office of Queen's and Lord Treasurer's Remembrancer existed, an office that went back into the medieval mists.

The first Remembrancers had been body servants of the early Scottish kings and queens, going everywhere with them. Their task had been to remember things for their ruler, unless it seemed wiser to forget—a literal blend of walking notebook and royal conscience.

Over the centuries, surviving union with England as an incidental, the Remembrancer's role had gradually evolved and developed, always growing.

Gaunt thought of lighting a cigarette, remembered he was trying to kick the habit, and turned to wondering what Falconer wanted this time. Falconer took his orders from the Remembrancer direct, and that could mean anything.

"He's clear," said Hannah. A light had come to life on her desk.

"Right." Gaunt lingered for a moment. "What's it about?"

She shook her head. But he caught what might have been a flicker of sympathy in her eyes. From Hannah, that wasn't good.

Leaving her, Gaunt went through into the inner office. Henry Falconer was standing at his window, looking out at the sunlight. He turned as Gaunt entered.

"Good morning," said Gaunt cheerfully.

"It is." Falconer gave an affable nod. A big, heavy-faced man in a dark business suit, white shirt, and golf club tie, he stood framed by the window like some Chamber of Commerce designed Buddha. "Shut the door and sit down. I've a job for you."

There was a chair placed ready on the receiving side of the senior administrative assistant's desk. Settling in it, Gaunt waited.

"Ah—done anything about getting another car?" asked Falconer. He spoke with the air of a man launching a carefully rehearsed pleasantry.

"Not yet, Henry." Gaunt gave him a lop-sided grin. He had a reasonable, if occasionally stormy relationship with Falconer. The man had his faults but was efficient—he also knew more about Gaunt than most people. "I might even get to like walking."

"Maybe you'll know better next time." Falconer stayed jovial. "Investments? With your luck, God help us all if you ever buy Government bonds."

He left the window and walked across the large, comfortably furnished room. Some of the items were Falconer's own, including a grandfather clock his wife wouldn't let him keep at home. He stopped at the clock, listened to its solid ticking for a few seconds, then went on and sat behind his desk.

"Now." There was a single green folder lying in front of him. Falconer fiddled with it. "This matter has—ah—been reviewed personally by the Remembrancer."

Gaunt nodded. But it could still mean anything. The modern Remembrancer, a senior-grade professional civil servant, was involved in most things that mattered. He might still be responsible for the security of the Scottish Crown jewels in their electronic fortress inside Edinburgh Castle, but he was also paymaster to every

Government department north of the border. He ran Company registrations, handled Treasure Trove, processed what was delicately called "State Intelligence," audited the Scottish law courts. In some situations he ran his own court of law. He could stick his nose into just about any situation.

"It comes under our remit." Falconer paused, hands clasped together, deliberately cracking his knuckles. "We've no option."

"Henry, get to it," said Gaunt softly. "Stop acting like a neurotic vulture."

"Coffee," said Falconer. He flicked his intercom switch and made quick, suitable noises to Hannah. Then he faced Gaunt again. "You know the maximum penalty for tax evasion?"

"Hanging?" Gaunt tried to shut out a memory of his last tax return.

"Treat it seriously," said Falconer indignantly. "A fine of three times the amount of tax due, plus a long spell behind bars." He scowled. "All right, nobody likes paying tax. Tax avoidance is legal, common sense. But tax evasion is fraud, a crime—and the rest of us are left having to pay more. Tax is—well, like being in a club."

"Except you can't resign," murmured Gaunt.

"Very funny." Falconer flicked open the folder in a way that made it slap the desk. "See if this amuses you. We've been landed with a tax evasion case, a nasty one. You're flying to Prague tomorrow."

"Where?" Gaunt stared at him.

"Prague. Czechoslovakia—unless the Reds have moved it recently." Falconer gave way to malicious pleasure at Gaunt's reaction, then recovered. "Confidentially, the Remembrancer doesn't like it. I don't. And . . ."

"And that makes three of us," said Gaunt.

"But it's settled." Falconer gestured at the folder. "Inland Revenue have a rotten apple in their barrel."

"I see." Gaunt drew a deep breath.

Things were suddenly both clearer and more complicated. Despite general opinion, tax collectors were human. They also had to pay tax like everyone else. And being human—he shrugged. Inland Revenue didn't like watchdogging its own. The Remembrancer's Office had that particular chore.

"Who's our man?" he asked resignedly.

"It's a her, not a he," said Falconer gloomily and ungrammatically. "Margaret Ann Dimond, widow, early forties, an administration expert on attachment to Centre One. She was a graduate entry, she has sixteen years' service and she's due for promotion. Or was—she appears to have stacked up more than sixty thousand pounds sterling in undeclared assets. All in the last two years."

"Well done, Margaret," said Gaunt.

"Her friends call her Maggie," said Falconer. "And don't ask the next question. She hasn't had any rich relatives die on her."

"If you say so. But how the hell does Prague come into it?" Gaunt paused, with a new suspicion he didn't like. "Look, Henry, I'm no kind of spy-catcher. No way."

"Agreed." Falconer used both hands in a quick, soothing gesture. "It's Prague because she keeps going there like a yo-yo. But we've been—ah—advised there's no apparent security angle."

"Who says?"

Falconer shrugged. "The usual people."

"Like that?" Gaunt sighed. "With their record, that's no comfort. What about Prague?"

"In here." Falconer tapped the folder. "She first went there on a holiday package, two years ago. Whatever happened, about a fortnight after she got back she moved out of a rented apartment and bought herself a country cottage. Cash, outright—except she told the people at work she was renting it."

"Playing careful," said Gaunt. "Is there a bank account?"

"Only one we know about in her name, needing each month's pay cheque like a blood transfusion," answered Falconer. He tapped the folder again. "She's Inland Revenue, she knows what she's doing. To date, our Mrs. Dimond has made six trips to Prague. Always on a package trip, always using annual leave—and always, afterwards, she seems to have been in the money again."

"But never waving it around?" Gaunt's interest was roused, despite his reservations. "Like she found a money tree?"

"Apparently," agreed Falconer. "Whatever she does, she always pays cash and keeps a low profile at work."

"Sensible," said Gaunt. "How did we find out?"

"An anonymous telephone call. It was made to this office direct. Someone obviously doesn't like her."

"Someone who knows we handle Inland Revenue internal nasties." Gaunt sucked his teeth. "I'd guess this 'someone' works beside her. Male voice?"

Falconer nodded.

"And she's due for promotion. So that gives us a disgruntled male chauvinist taxman—"

"The female of the species would probably have cut her throat," said Falconer. "Anyway, we've had people working on it locally since we heard. That was a few weeks ago. But now she's off again —we had another telephone call yesterday, same male voice. The information checks out. She made a sudden application for leave, and it was due her."

"Tomorrow?" Gaunt raised an eyebrow.

"She leaves. Another package trip, for one week. You're on the same flight out of London, same package, same hotel."

There was a tap on the door. It opened and Hannah came in, carrying a small tray. She dumped a mug of coffee in front of Gaunt, then went round and placed the tray beside Falconer. The senior administrative assistant had a cup and saucer, with matching cream jug and sugar bowl. Falconer thanked her with a smile, a smile that lingered on his heavy face until his secretary had gone out and the door had closed again.

"Your mind is showing, Henry," said Gaunt.

"I'm fortunate. She's a damned efficient woman," said Falconer with bland pomposity. He cleared his throat. "Prague . . ."

"Prague," said Gaunt wearily. He nursed his coffee mug in both hands and took a cautious gulp. "What about the Czechs or any stray Russians?"

"You've a tourist visa, you're travelling on your own passport." Falconer beamed at him. "They love tourists—they need the foreign currency. You won't have problems."

Gaunt glared at him. "You guarantee it?"

"Why not?" Falconer added sugar and cream to his coffee and stirred it carefully. "Anyway, we haven't time to do it any other way. Make any kind of official approach and they'd take months— then say no, and either shoot the woman or give her a medal." He sipped his coffee. "Don't contact our Embassy people unless it becomes critical. Try—ah—not to create any incidents. Just keep an eye on what the woman does, come back, and report."

"Anything else?" Gaunt didn't hide the sarcasm in his voice.

"One thing that should make things easier for you." Falconer gave his coffee another experimental stir. "There's an industrial trade fair running in Prague. The Czechs will have plenty of other foreigners around." He leaned back. "It's a beautiful city, Jonathan. Look on the bright side, eh?"

"Like what?"

"Well, a chance to forget some of your other problems." Falconer stopped short and flushed, suddenly embarrassed. "I—well, what I meant was—"

"Present problems?" Gaunt bridged the awkward gap for him, knowing it was genuine.

"Yes. Of course." Falconer hesitated. "Everything else is—?"

"Fine," said Gaunt. It was reasonably true, most of the time. He nodded at the folder. "Let me see what we've got."

Relieved, Falconer pushed it over.

It was another fifteen minutes before Gaunt left the room, the folder under one arm. Hannah was at her desk, and looked up.

"Tell me something," she said, frowning. "Have you got another car yet?"

"No. That's today's bulletin." He grinned at her. "But maybe soon—why?"

"I saw your expense sheet going through," she said accusingly. "You're still charging mileage."

"Foot mileage," he explained solemnly. "Shoe leather, Hannah—it's energy conservation."

She glared after him as he disappeared along the corridor, then turned to the intercom on her desk, touching a switch.

"He's gone," she said. "You wanted to know."

In his room, Henry Falconer settled deeper in his chair for a moment. The sun coming in the window picked up the smoothly polished case of his grandfather clock, highlighting every detail of the fine wood. It was an old clock. He wasn't really sure how old, but some day he'd try and find out.

Sighing, he sat upright, reached for the private line telephone on his desk, and dialled a number.

"I've told him," he said.

"Good," said a voice. "He'll do it?"

"Yes." Falconer hesitated, frowning. "But—"

"Second thoughts?" asked the voice, with a touch of amusement.

"No," said Falconer indignantly. "But if we'd told him more—"

"It's safer this way," said the voice. "Goodbye."

The line went dead. Hanging up, Falconer lumbered to his feet. It was time to report to the Remembrancer.

Jonathan Gaunt had a call of his own to make. Back in his cubby-hole office, he dropped the Maggie Dimond folder on his desk, settled into his chair with a wince, then reached for the telephone. He changed his mind, took the spare bottle of pain-killer tablets from his top drawer, and swallowed one.

Half-way through the interview with Falconer, he'd felt the start of another familiar, low-grade ache in his back. They'd been coming almost daily for about a week, probably linked with the amount of walking he was doing.

He cursed. The army medics had said he'd never be totally free from them, and so far they'd been totally right. His grey-green eyes clouded at the memory, and he glanced at the Maggie Dimond folder.

Two years ago, roughly when she'd made that first visit to Prague, he'd been Lieutenant Jonathan Gaunt, Parachute Regiment, proud of his platoon, his red beret and the parachute wings above his battledress pocket.

Two years ago he'd led his platoon on an exercise jump; a simple, routine jump out of a transport aircraft making a low-speed pass over a mock objective at three thousand feet. But Lieutenant Gaunt had tumbled out of the sky with a partial "chute failure"—every paratrooper's nightmare suddenly come to reality. He should have died. Sometimes, in the long months in a British military hospital, he'd wished it had been that way. A broken back mended slowly.

Afterwards there had been a Medical Board, the Army's formal goodbye, a disability pension—and the pain-killers.

"The hell with it," he said aloud. Being morose didn't help. He'd learned that along the way.

Reaching for the telephone again, he got an outside line and dialled. With what he had in mind he needed transport and John Milton, stockbroker, seemed the best bet among his friends. When he was connected, Milton came on the line after a moment's switchboard delay.

"I need a favour," said Gaunt without preliminaries. "Your wheels, John—just for tonight. Work."

"No problem." Milton was the type who didn't ask unnecessary questions. "Pick up the keys here. The tank's full—I want it back that way."

"Thanks." Gaunt grinned at the mouthpiece. "And I won't make tomorrow night's poker session. I'm on the move again."

"One way or return?" asked Milton dryly. He chuckled. "I've got some news about those comic shares you bought. After preferred creditors, you'll maybe get twenty per cent—eventually."

"Don't expect me to cheer," Gaunt told him grimly.

"It could be worse." Milton made a sympathetic noise. "Look, maybe this will help bind the wounds. You didn't hear it from me, but I've a rich punter suddenly buying a certain whisky share on an inside whisper about a free scrip issue. If you want a fast buy-and-sell ride on his coat-tails, blind—"

"I'll let you know." Gaunt said goodbye, hung up, and eyed the folder again.

Maggie Dimond worked at Centre One. A massive computer beehive located about forty miles from Edinburgh, in the new town of East Kilbride, Centre One processed the tax assessments of about half the wage-earning population of Scotland. Maggie Dimond's cottage was on the outskirts of East Kilbride.

There was plenty about her in the folder. But it was cold, official report style. If he had to trail the woman around Prague, Gaunt wanted something different. A taste of how she lived, the personality behind those report sheets. There was only one way to do that.

The pain-killer was beginning to work. He took out his cigarettes, lit one, and sat back with his eyes half-closed.

Being dumped into a puzzle like where the Dimond woman got her money, with the Czech possibility, was the kind of situation that made working for the Remembrancer almost a fascination. He grimaced, remembering Falconer's embarrassment after saying Prague would let him "forget some of his other problems."

The senior administrative assistant was that old-fashioned item, a gentleman. He still embarrassed easily, and he knew about Patti, the rest of Gaunt's past.

She'd been young, blond, and beautiful. As Mrs. Gaunt, she visited hospital faithfully. She'd waited until the day after his discharge before quietly telling Gaunt he could add a broken marriage to the list.

The tensions had been there, long before his last jump. Neither of them had been particularly to blame—they'd agreed on that. Patti wasn't the first girl who'd married a uniform and a pair of parachute wings. With those gone—well, at least there weren't children. The parting had been civilized.

She'd married again within a few months. Her new husband was a prosperous, likeable man, who tried to be friendly in an awkward way any time Gaunt met them. Patti had survived without problems.

But Gaunt had suddenly learned how much he'd lost all round. He'd drifted, out of work, living on that disability pension, not particularly giving a damn. Until someone he still didn't know by name had remembered that the onetime Lieutenant Gaunt had spent a few university terms studying law and accountancy before deciding to be a soldier.

There had been a summons to the Remembrancer's Office. An interview. When it finished, he'd almost reluctantly found himself on the payroll.

Within weeks, he'd discovered he was doing a job he enjoyed. Living again. Still with the occasional sweating nightmare, falling out of the sky, screaming in his mind, waking just before he hit the ground.

But living.

Prague. He drew lightly on the cigarette again. Getting a short-notice visa without creating fuss couldn't have been easy. The Queen's and Lord Treasurer's Remembrancer had some interesting contacts.

Even in Prague. Mentioned in the Department's usual laconic style, his briefing included a "safe" contact name, for emergency use only. But that was in the future. Stubbing what was left of the cigarette, Gaunt pulled the folder towards him again and got down to work.

He spent the rest of the morning working through the evidence in the folder. Then, getting a messenger to take it back to Falconer, he had a sandwich and coffee lunch in a snack-bar off George Street.

When Gaunt returned, there was a package on his desk. It contained his air tickets, a cash advance on expenses, and his passport. Flicking through the pages, he checked the brand-new visa stamp in red and green ink headed *Ceskovenska Vizum,* then opened the envelope which had been lying at the bottom of the package. It was a colour photograph of Maggie Dimond, an obvious blow-up from some acquired group shot.

Gaunt considered the photograph for a long time. It was his first positive step to seeing his target as someone real.

Cold print had told him that Maggie Dimond, born London, age forty-three, widow of a university lecturer, was an Honours history graduate. Some business administration qualifications had come later. On her tax return papers there were no listed dependants. She claimed normal personal tax allowances, her union membership, and two life policies.

But the photograph showed him a woman very different from what he'd expected.

She had long, copper-coloured hair, swept back at the sides. Her face was strong, with large blue eyes and a wide, generous mouth. The photograph showed her wearing a cocktail dress and she had a good figure. But the photograph had caught something else, a smile which had an underlying thoughtfulness.

He'd taken Maggie Dimond's intelligence for granted. Women still had to fight their way up each rung of the Civil Service ladder. But now he felt sure of something else—she was nobody's fool.

It wouldn't make his task any easier.

He waited until about 5 P.M., left the building and walked the few hundred yards through the city centre to John Milton's office. The stockbroker was in a meeting with clients but came out for a moment. A small, plump man in a well-cut business suit, he greeted Gaunt with a cheerful nod.

"Be gentle with her," he pleaded, handing over his car keys. "She's parked round the corner. When you're finished, leave her outside my house. Okay?"

"Wrapped in a blanket," promised Gaunt.

"Right." Milton lowered his voice to a murmur. "What about those whisky shares, Jonny? You've no credit rating problems here."

Gaunt pursed his lips and resisted temptation. "Maybe when I get back."

"From where?" asked Milton.

"Prague."

Milton raised an eyebrow. "The Trade Fair?"

"Partly," said Gaunt.

"Interesting." Milton brightened. "How about taking my mother-in-law along? Swap her for a tractor, or something useful."

Gaunt laughed, shook his head, and left.

Milton's car, a black BMW, was where he'd said. Getting in, Gaunt adjusted the seat, checked the controls, and fed one of the stockbroker's music tapes into the cassette player on the dashboard. Then he set the car moving.

The tape was an orchestral dirge, badly recorded. He swapped it for a Spanish flamenco collection at the first set of traffic lights. After that, there were no problems. The drive west was smooth and uneventful, out along the M8 motorway towards Glasgow in moderate traffic.

It was 6 P.M. with dusk greying in when Gaunt left the motorway on the East Kilbride turn-off. Another ten minutes, and the black BMW was cruising through the town's outskirts.

East Kilbride was a post World War Two creation of bricks and concrete dumped on what had once been pleasant farmland. One of its few real landmarks was the tall, slab-like Centre One tax building.

Gaunt stopped close by its high rise of large, brightly lit and uncurtained windows. Centre One stayed that way day and night, a totally controlled environment for its tax-gathering data banks. He was more interested in the fact that the staff car-park was empty and the offices behind the windows were deserted.

Maggie Dimond's cottage was called Low Well and was outside the village of Eaglesham, about five miles on. He checked one of Milton's road maps, then drove on again. At Eaglesham, a small, old village which looked fashionable and expensive, dusk was giving way to darkness as he saw the signpost he wanted.

It led the BMW down a narrow side-road. Gaunt drove slowly, the car's headlights sweeping fields and farmland as the little road wound on, potholed and liberally littered with cattle dung. The car's underside took its share of punishment from both while it passed several cottages and a couple of farm steadings.

Then, as the BMW rounded another bend, the headlights lit a pair of white gates and the sign Low Well.

He went past at a crawl. A short length of driveway led from the gates to a small, single-storey cottage with a high-pitched roof which

was a dark silhouette in the wan moonlight. The cottage was occupied. Lights showed behind its glass front door and one of the windows. Two cars were parked nose to tail in the driveway, a small Ford station wagon and, behind it, nearest the road, a white Jaguar coupe. The Jaguar had been left with its sidelights on.

A farm track met the road another hundred yards along. Gaunt stopped the BMW, reversed in, then switched off engine and lights. He left the cassette player running, the volume turned low, and watched the cottage.

He'd driven through with a vague purpose in mind. See where anyone lived, go from there to the nearest inn or bar, pick up some gossip and the results could be useful. If that failed, there were other ways—including the local constable. Country cops knew about most people, at least a little, and were ready to talk once they saw identification.

But the Jaguar might mean something else.

The tape ran out. He fed another in and let the soft music wash over him. A car murmured past on the road, but nothing else moved.

Several minutes passed, then he stiffened. The lights had gone out in the cottage, leaving it in total darkness. He heard a car engine start up. The white Jaguar reversed out onto the road, rear lights gleaming.

Another rasp from the engine and the Jaguar pulled away, heading back the way he'd arrived. Cursing under his breath, Gaunt set the BMW moving and followed, keeping his distance.

The driver ahead was in no hurry and it was a short journey. The Jaguar coupe murmured into Eaglesham village and swung off the road into a hotel parking lot. Gaunt followed and tucked the BMW into an empty slot some distance away. Then he watched as a man and woman got out of the other car. They walked across to a brightly lit side-door and went into the hotel.

He had a clear view as they passed through the pool of light. The woman was Maggie Dimond. She wore a dark-green cocktail dress and had a white wool stole over her shoulders. Her companion, a balding, middle-aged man, was below medium height but heavily built. He was dressed in a blazer and checked sports trousers.

Gaunt gave them a couple of minutes then climbed out of the

BMW. Going over, he found the Jaguar was locked; but it was the latest V-twelve model, only a few months old, expensive in anyone's currency. He made a mental note of the registration number then turned towards the hotel.

Windows along one side gave a view into the softly lit cocktail bar. Maggie Dimond and her escort were already seated at a table, talking earnestly with their heads close together. The man's broad face had a deep scar on one cheek, an old wound which acted like a barrier when he gave a sudden smile at something she said to him. Easing back a little, Gaunt switched his attention to Maggie Dimond. Her photograph hadn't lied. She was an attractive woman, taller than her companion, and she was doing most of the talking, pointing a finger for emphasis, her eyes sparkling.

The conversation broke off as a waiter brought drinks to their table. He also offered the couple menu cards, and they studied them.

Gaunt waited. If Maggie Dimond was eating out, that gave him more of an opportunity than he'd expected.

He was in luck. The waiter returned again and the couple began to order. Humming under his breath, Gaunt went back to the BMW and started it up.

Five minutes later he was back at Low Well cottage. This time he left the BMW at the side of the road, close in under the shadow of a hedge. The car's black body merged into the darkness and when he looked back after a few paces he could hardly see it.

The cottage was still unlit. Walking up the driveway, past the empty Ford station wagon, he made his way round to the rear of the little house. Breaking and entering wasn't part of any regular Remembrancer's Department remit, but it wasn't the Remembrancer who was being sent to Prague.

The kitchen door was uncompromisingly solid wood with the kind of keyhole that went with a modern double-mortice lock. Gaunt moved on under the faint moonlight, then stopped and frowned, instinct telling him something was wrong.

A small extension had been built at the back of the cottage. It included a full-length glass patio door, and the door was already open a tempting few inches. Warily, ready for anything, Gaunt crept forward. He reached the door, ran his hand down the smooth edge of the frame, and felt a rough edge of metal where the lock had been forced.

Easing the door wider on its runners he stayed where he was, listening. A faint sound reached him. Then a glow of light moved, further back in the cottage.

Someone with a torch. Maggie Dimond already had an uninvited visitor.

Stepping into the room, Gaunt gave his eyes a moment to grow accustomed to the deeper darkness, then tiptoed forward. Brushing against partly unseen furniture, he reached an archway at the other side and found himself in a small hallway, the start of the original cottage.

The torchlight was coming from the next room. The beam moved again, showing what was obviously a bedroom. The man behind it, an indistinct shape, left wherever he'd been and crossed to a dressing table. There was a low squeak as a drawer was opened, and the figure began rummaging through its contents.

Three silent steps took Gaunt to within touching range.

"Police," he said curtly. "Stay like that."

The man jerked, then went into a scrabbling turn. Gaunt grabbed him, the torch went out, and they collided in the darkness.

A hand clawed at his face. A blow with the torch hit him on the shoulder. In no mood for niceties, Gaunt brought his knee up hard into the man's crotch, heard an explosive whoop of pain, and followed it with a chopping blow with the side of his hand which, though it missed the man's throat, still hit him across the mouth.

Overbalancing, they went down together, fell across the bed, then from there fell to the floor. Rolling, struggling in the dark, they collided with a small table and it crashed over.

His opponent was strong, desperate. His hands made a grab at Gaunt's throat and tightened. Gaunt swung his fist, felt as much as heard the smack as it connected with the man's jaw, and the grip on his throat relaxed. He tore free, seizing the intruder's shoulders, and went for a head butt.

He didn't make it. Suddenly the room lights were switched on. A voice behind him gave a hoarse shout—then something hard hit him on the back of the head.

Dazed, stupefied by the blow, Gaunt sprawled on the floor.

Dimly, the thought penetrated that there had been two men. A boot thudded into his ribs, hard. He heard a low mutter of voices, then he was kicked again.

But it stopped there, and the room became silent. Groaning, he rolled on his side and looked up. He was alone, the men had gone.

Still dazed, Gaunt got to his feet and staggered back through the cottage to the patio door. He went out into the night air, hesitated, then heard a car starting up and headed down the driveway towards the road at a shambling run.

Headlamps glared from a point a distance beyond where he'd left his own borrowed vehicle. Then the car began moving, accelerating hard. It came round a bend before the cottage. A moment later there was a brief squeal of brakes, a loud rasp of metal on metal, then a fresh rasp of acceleration as the strange car kept going.

The tail-lights vanished from sight. Head still throbbing, Gaunt left the driveway and walked slowly towards the BMW.

The bodywork had been raked along one side, as if attacked by a giant tin-opener. John Milton's pride and joy was going to need some expensive panel-beating surgery.

For the moment that was incidental. Taking a deep breath, Gaunt went back to the cottage. Going in, switching on the lights, he looked around. It was a well-furnished home, modernized, comfortable.

A small desk had been forced open in the living-room and papers scattered. Nearby, a drinks cupboard had been opened and an empty bottle lay on the carpet beside an apparently abandoned silver dish.

But that was all. Except for the bedroom, the rest of the cottage looked untouched. It was as if a petty thief had broken in, had grabbed the first valuables he'd seen, then had taken fright and bolted.

What had really happened had been something different. The men he'd disturbed hadn't been amateurs. They'd been searching the cottage, searching carefully and neatly, leaving only the picture they wanted, enough to explain the forced patio door.

And if they'd found anything, it had gone with them.

The papers in the desk were domestic bills and told him nothing. Gaunt checked his head in a mirror, explored the beginnings of a large bump with his fingertips, then decided it was time to leave. He went through the cottage again, switching out lights, wiping the switches with a handkerchief, and returned to the BMW.

A few miles later, he telephoned Henry Falconer's home number from a roadside call-box. Falconer's wife answered, then the senior administrative assistant came on the line.

"You could have picked a better time," said Falconer, crustily. "At my age, a man deserves his after-dinner nap. What's wrong?"

"Several things." Gaunt gave him a cut-down account of what had happened, punctuated by an occasional dubious grunt from the other end.

"I won't ask what your own intentions were," said Falconer heavily at the finish. "But—yes, I'm interested. Do nothing more and stay clear of the police. Give me the Jaguar's registration number again—and anything you remember about the man with Mrs. Dimond."

Gaunt did.

"Nothing on the two—ah—other gentlemen?"

"Just that they've a dented car with black paint sticking to it," said Gaunt.

"Which hardly helps," Falconer told him. "Go home. I'll call you."

The line went dead.

It still wasn't late when Gaunt got back to Edinburgh. He drove round to John Milton's house, parked the BMW outside, then rang the doorbell. There was no one at home and he was glad. After pushing the car keys through the letter-box, he walked away and caught a bus at the end of the road.

Twenty minutes later Gaunt was in his own two-room bachelor apartment on the east side of the city. His first priority was a large whisky, which he drank at a gulp. He made himself a sandwich with some cold meat he found in the refrigerator, washed it down with coffee, then sat and smoked a cigarette.

The telephone rang just as he finished the cigarette. When he answered, John Milton's voice rasped in his ear.

"What the hell happened to my car?" demanded the outraged stockbroker.

"One of those parking bumps," began Gaunt. "Sorry . . ."

"A bump?" Milton's voice climbed hysterically. "My God, you could have done less damage with a sledge-hammer. What do I tell my insurance company?"

"I said sorry," soothed Gaunt. "Get it fixed and send me the bill." What would happen when that item turned up in his expenses was something else, but it could wait. "Believe me, it won't look so bad in daylight."

"You'll get the bill," promised Milton, only slightly mollified. "What kind of parking accident leaves a car looking like it's been in a war?"

"It was just bad luck," said Gaunt. "Would I lie to you?"

"Only if it mattered," said Milton bleakly. "Damn you anyway— and you owe me a drink when you get back."

Gaunt laughed, said goodbye, and hung up.

He was packing his travel bag when the telephone rang again. This time it was Henry Falconer.

"How's the head?" asked Falconer.

"Still attached." Gaunt fingered the bump with his free hand. "Henry, you know what happened. Give me a straight answer. Have I got the full story?"

"About the Dimond woman?" Falconer made a throat-clearing noise over the line. "All we know. Of course, if there are—ah—side issues, they don't concern us."

Gaunt swore under his breath. "Meaning?"

"That we're only concerned with a tax evasion," countered Falconer. "My word on it."

"Tell that to the two characters I met tonight," said Gaunt. "All right, go on."

"We've an owner for the white Jaguar," said Falconer. "He matches the description of the man who was with the Dimond woman—he's Matthew Garr, a Swiss national, normally based in London. There's a Home Office file on him, interest only—no convictions."

"Any Czech links?"

"None known," admitted Falconer. "He's a merchant banker with some rather strange friends—"

"Political?"

"More criminal," said Falconer. He broke off as a woman's voice sounded in the background, then came back on the line. "I've to

take the dog for a walk. But I'll call again in the morning, before
you leave. Good night."

Jonathan Gaunt slept well that night. Perhaps because he was
tired, perhaps because that usually happened when outside tensions
were pressing in. There was no nightmare, no need for a pain-killer
tablet.

The alarm clock at his bedside woke him at seven. He had shaved
and showered and was dressing when the telephone rang again.

"Good morning," said Falconer briskly. "Something interesting for
you. Mrs. Dimond hasn't bothered to tell the police she had a break-
in. But she spent the night at home, and left by car for the airport
about five minutes ago."

Maggie Dimond would be flying the Glasgow shuttle to London,
just as his own travel schedule began with the Edinburgh shuttle
flight down. The Prague flight originated at London Heathrow.

"Was she alone?" Gaunt didn't ask Falconer's source. But he knew
someone had spent a cold, lonely night just watching.

"Apparently." Falconer gave a mild chuckle. "No sign of Garr or
his Jaguar, anyway. It must be a purely business relationship. Good-
looking woman, from her photograph. Ah—"

"They come worse," said Gaunt.

"Well, have a good trip," said Falconer. He paused, then sounded
almost embarrassed. "Just go, keep your eyes open, then come back.
Don't stir up trouble. You understand?"

"No," said Gaunt, "but I hope somebody does."

He hung up and reached for his jacket.

CHAPTER 2

As usual, most of the passengers on the early morning British Airways shuttle from Edinburgh to London clutched executive briefcases and were trying hard to look awake. Some studied the financial pages with a glazed intensity, but Jonathan Gaunt didn't feel in that kind of mood. He stayed with the sports news and the comic strips.

There was a tail wind. It cut the flight time to an hour, then the Trident jet touched down at Heathrow in a gray drizzle of rain. Once inside the domestic terminal, he collected his travel bag from the luggage carousel and checked the arrivals board.

The Glasgow–London shuttle still hadn't landed and had left behind schedule for "technical reasons." He grimaced at the vague airline parlance, which could mean anything from an engine falling off to the flight-deck crew forgetting to turn up, but the delay suited his plans.

Gaunt crossed through to the international terminal and located the Czechoslovakian State Airlines desk. A steady trickle of passengers were already checking in for the Prague flight. He stood back, staying on the edge of a swarm of college students laying siege to a charter company's desk. They were bound for Yugoslavia. From the noise they were making, Yugoslavia would remember the occasion.

He waited, smoked a cigarette, watched more passengers arrive for the Prague flight, then at last saw Maggie Dimond.

The copper-haired widow had left any remnant of her Inland Revenue image at home. Dressed in tailored bottle-green jacket and skirt with a white sweater, wearing a large-brimmed bottle-green hat, a tweed coat hanging loose across her shoulders, she walked confidently through the confusion. Close behind her came a porter with two red-canvas suitcases.

Picking up his travel bag, Gaunt eased forward to join her in the check-in line.

"Jonathan." The deep voice came from behind him as a hand gripped his arm. "What are you doing here?"

He stopped, glanced round, and the man still holding his arm gave a friendly and, as usual, slightly awkward grin.

"Fleeing the country," said Gaunt. He tried to keep an eye on Maggie Dimond's progress while they shook hands. "How about you?"

Mentally, he felt like cursing.

But he had only one ex-wife and Eric Garfield was her new husband. Broad-shouldered, heavily built, Garfield was about forty-five and sober with it. But hard not to like. Patti's choice of an older man had surprised him initially. Maybe that was what she needed. Garfield also had money, worked hard for it, and enjoyed spending it.

"Making double sure one of my people gets on her flight," said Garfield briskly. He smiled at an attractive, dark-haired girl standing watching them. "Carol, come and meet a—uh—a friend of mine." He completed the introduction as she joined them. "Carol Marek— Jonathan Gaunt. Carol's one of my research and development team."

Maggie Dimond had reached the check-in desk. There were two other people now behind her. Gaunt surrendered to the situation. Carol Marek was slightly over medium height, probably in her late twenties. She wore fawn corduroy trousers, the legs tucked into tan, high-heeled leather boots. Beneath an Icelandic wool jacket with a hood, she had a dark blue shirt, open enough at the neck to give a glimpse of a thin gold chain which dipped down into the hollow between her breasts.

"Heading for Prague?" asked Gaunt politely.

"Yes." The girl's brown eyes held a suspicion of a twinkle. "You?"

He nodded.

"Splendid." Garfield made a pleased noise. "You can keep an eye on her, eh?"

"My pleasure." Gaunt saw a twitch of amusement on the dark-haired girl's lips. Eric Garfield might have built up a little Scottish-based electronics and computer software company into Trellux Components, as modern as any in its field, but he had some old-fashioned notions. "If the lady doesn't mind."

"No." The twitch became a chuckle. "I like company. Are you in our line of business, Mr. Gaunt?"

"He's some odd kind of civil servant," explained Garfield quickly. "I'm sending Carol to take in a Trade Fair for me, but what about you—business or pleasure, Jonathan?"

"Fifty-fifty." Maggie Dimond had finished at the check-in and was leaving. Smoothly, Gaunt slid into the story he'd agreed on with Henry Falconer. "I'm due some days off. My boss is on a government-backed exhibitions committee, the kind always looking for new ideas." He shrugged. "Provided I prowl around the Trade Fair layout a couple of times, the rest of the stay is my own."

"At the taxpayer's expense." Garfield's frown showed he didn't totally approve. "I suppose that's reasonable—if it doesn't happen too often." He glanced at his wrist-watch as he spoke. "I'm due at a meeting in the city this morning. Carol, if you don't mind, I'll leave now."

"You'd better," she agreed. "I don't want to be blamed if you're late."

"Right." Garfield nodded with a touch of relief. "Cable as arranged, or telephone if there's a problem." He turned to Gaunt. "It was good to see you again. Enjoy your—ah—break."

"Thanks." Gaunt stopped him. "How's Patti?"

"Fine. She's"—Garfield hesitated, then gave a quick, almost nervous smile—"yes, fine. Couldn't be better. I'll tell her we met and we'll be in touch."

He gave them both a perfunctory nod, touched Carol Marek's arm, then hurried off. In a moment, he was lost in the terminal's bustle.

"There are worse bosses," said Carol Marek with affection. "In fact, that's the trouble. It's hard to get mad at him."

Gaunt grinned at her. "He seems to trust you."

"I know my job," she said. "What he doesn't realize is that I don't need to be handed over to someone as if I was a stray dog." She eyed him steadily. "We can say goodbye if you want."

"No." Gaunt rubbed a thumb along his chin. "I was going to try another approach—bribery. Suppose I buy you a drink?"

Carol Marek gave a slow smile and nodded.

They went through the check-in formalities, followed by customs, immigration, and the usual security search. Carol Marek had a British passport, which left him wondering about a faint, hard-to-place accent in her voice.

It was still puzzling Gaunt when they entered the international departures lounge. He looked around, decided it was too big and too busy to even think of locating Maggie Dimond, and steered a way through towards the bar. Carol Marek ordered a brandy, he settled for a beer, and they took their drinks over to a vacant table.

"Have you been in Prague before?" she asked, once they'd settled.

He shook his head. "You?"

"Yes." She sipped her drink. "A few times. I've relatives out there."

"Marek—" he raised a questioning eyebrow.

"My father is Czech—or was. He got out in the fifties." She wrinkled her nose. "Then he married an Irish girl, which makes quite a mixture. They called me Carol because I was born on Christmas Day and they both went sentimental about it. Anyway, he took out British citizenship and after that we went to Prague a few times. Before the Russians really took over." She sat back. "Eric Garfield said you were some kind of civil servant. Exactly what kind?"

"The nine-to-five variety that does everything in triplicate," he said vaguely. "But we get an inflation-proof pension if we last out. How long have you been with Eric Garfield?"

"About a year." She nursed the glass between her hands and gave the brandy a gentle swirl. "Before that I was with another electronics company. But he offered more money."

"He buys the best," said Gaunt. "Do you speak Czech?"

"Enough." She grimaced across the table. "That's probably the only reason he allowed me to go on my own. We flew down from Glasgow together this morning and all the way it was a non-stop lecture—what to do, what not to do."

"He means well," soothed Gaunt.

"I know that," she agreed. "But sooner or later, if I'm going to keep working for him, he'll have to realize—"

"That you don't need a nursemaid?"

"More." Carol Marek took a gulp of her brandy. "A woman can have a genuine edge on men in the microchip and electronics game. It's like—"

"Embroidery?" suggested Gaunt innocently.

"Go to hell." She grinned at him. "There just happen to be some concepts the female mind is more able to grasp." She turned, looking round for the departure board. "How long now till we get this plane?"

The board said forty minutes. Less than half that time had passed when Gaunt's name was called between flight announcements. The voice on the speaker system asked him to report to the information desk.

When he got there a clerk asked for his passport, glanced at it, then gave a faint nod to a man standing nearby.

The man came over, picked up one of the leaflets on the desk, and began studying it.

"I've a message for you, Mr. Gaunt," he murmured, not looking up. "Customs got a down-the-line request this morning to check a Mrs. Dimond's flight baggage, then let you know. We did. Nothing unusual—same with the personal search at security. As far as we're concerned she's clean."

He tucked the leaflet into a pocket and drifted off. Stony-faced, Gaunt waited a moment longer before he retrieved his passport.

Someone in Edinburgh had had a last-minute thought, a reasonable one. In a negative way it had been worthwhile—and had also brought his mind back to what mattered.

"Some idiotic tangle about my ticket," he explained when he got back to Carol Marek. "It's straightened out." He indicated her empty glass. "We've time for another."

"Please. But call this one medicinal." She looked up at him with a slightly ashamed expression and fingered the thin gold chain at her neck. "I'm one of the league of white-knuckled air travellers—I'd rather go on a broomstick."

He thought about that and smiled. Carol Marek would have made a fairly spectacular witch.

Czechoslovak Air Lines' flight OK 252 boarded on time and took off on schedule. It was a shabby turbo-fan Tupolev 154, less than half its one hundred and sixty seats filled, and the cabin staff made it plain that wasn't their worry.

Gaunt's luck was in. He and Carol Marek had one three-seat section to themselves and Maggie Dimond sat on her own just across the aisle and one row ahead. The nearest of the other passengers were a middle-aged couple, husband and wife, who were two rows behind Maggie Dimond, and a thin, dark-haired man who had the window seat in front of Carol.

Apart from the cabin signs and the rapid burst of Czech from the cabin address system before take-off, it was a flight pretty much like any other. After climbing fast out of Heathrow, the Tupolev levelled out and headed east on a curving flight-plan which would take it over Belgium and both German states.

It was a six-hundred-mile, one-and-a-half-hour flight, from one style of living to another. Talking to Carol, watching the cabin staff serve drinks and a meal, Gaunt gave an occasional glance in Maggie Dimond's direction.

She seemed totally at ease, reading a magazine and smoking an occasional cigarette. She ordered a vodka aperitif, then had red wine with her meal. If she had the slightest interest in any of her fellow passengers, she didn't show it. Gaunt shifted his gaze. The dark-haired man in front appeared to be dozing. Across the aisle, the middle-aged couple, from the English Midlands by their accents, were hard at work on a book of crossword puzzles.

He felt a nudge in his side and realized Carol had been speaking.

"Sorry." He gave her an apologetic grimace. "I missed that."

"Twice," she agreed, amused. "All I wanted to know is where you're staying. What hotel?"

"In Prague?" The answer had been chosen for him, matching Maggie Dimond's package. "The Smetana—do you know it?"

She nodded. "By reputation—it's been built since the last time I was out. But Trellux booked me in there too. Reports are it's big, one of the best they've got, and usually full of Russians."

"The tourist type?" asked Gaunt.

"Tourists with brief-cases," she said flatly, and gave a shrug when he raised an eyebrow. "Look, make up your own mind about things. I'm biased—and I've heard my father talk too often. He's safe, with a British passport, but he has stopped visiting." Her lips tightened. "You know the biggest change? The way people laugh—not out loud any more, and not very often if there's a stranger around."

"They have it rough," said Gaunt quietly.

"Your average Czech? No." She surprised him, shaking her head. "Not rough, unless they make trouble. They're just getting on with living in a way they don't like. Because there's nothing they can do about it, nothing anyone else will."

She fell silent, and Gaunt decided to leave things that way.

Maggie Dimond left her seat only once during the flight, for a brief visit to one of the toilets aft. On her way back, she collided with the dark-haired man who was heading in the same direction, and she gave Gaunt an apologetic smile as she brushed against his shoulder.

The Tupolev had begun losing height. There were occasional glimpses of wooded hills, and thin, ribbon-like roads linking tiny villages, then the seat-belt and no-smoking signs came on.

They came in through cloud to a tight, fast landing which had the dark-haired girl beside him grip the arms of her seat. She let out a long sigh of relief as the aircraft vibrated with reverse thrust then slowed.

"Now all I've got to do is get back again," she said wryly. "You know, I even tried a relaxation course as a cure."

"And?"

"I decided half the class were pilots in disguise." Carol shook her head in disgust. "So I live with it."

The Tupolev taxied in, heading for a long, slab-sided terminal building decorated with an abundance of banners, Russian flags and Czech flags. Civilian aircraft from both sides of the Iron Curtain were parked on the apron strip but over to their left was the other side of the coin. A soldier in a fur hat and long greatcoat stood sentry beside three MIG jet fighters. He had a rifle. The MIG jets, drab and menacing in their camouflage paint, had the Red Star on their wings.

They stopped some distance from the terminal and were shepherded out of the Tupolev and across to a waiting bus. The wind was light but with an icy edge, the temperature several degrees colder than they'd left in Britain, and no one lingered. Two armed police in brown uniforms, one with a machine-pistol slung over his shoulder, watched with disinterest from a small, open scout-car until the bus doors closed.

The scout-car followed the bus to the terminal entrance, where there were twinned Russian and Czech flags. A long banner, lettered in gold, read in English: "Welcome to the Czechoslovak Socialist Republic."

The welcome began inside.

One by one, the queue of passengers from the Tupolev had to pass through three consecutive check-points manned by uniformed officials. Each passport and travel document was examined in stony silence, then thrust back into the owner's hand. The atmosphere was polite but chill, the silence only broken by the shuffling of feet, the total effect demoralizing.

Gaunt was glad to emerge on the other side, in the baggage hall. Carol was already through and talking to the middle-aged couple who had been opposite them on the flight. Maggie Dimond was still back in the slow-moving queue, carrying her hat, the tweed coat across her shoulders again.

"Hello there." The middle-aged man greeted him good-humouredly then nodded towards the check-points. "Don't take chances, do they?"

"It seemed that way," admitted Gaunt.

"That's life, I suppose—and business these days." The man was balding, plump, and slightly below medium height. He had a round, ruddy face, a small ginger moustache, and a gaudy taste in ties. "Ever tried to get through Kennedy Airport on a bad day? That's no picnic." He eyed Gaunt brightly. "Over for the Trade Fair?"

Gaunt nodded.

"I thought so." The small moustache twitched with satisfaction. "Didn't I, Helen?"

The woman beside him, plain and mousy-haired, his match in height and build, nodded dutifully but without particular interest. She wore a wool dress which looked as though it had shrunk in the wash, and she carried a fur-trimmed leather coat which had seen better days.

"I'm John Alford. This is my wife, Helen." Alford winked as he spoke. "She's my secretary this trip, tax deductible."

Gaunt completed the introductions, having no alternative. But his real attention had switched to the other side of the baggage hall.

The same thin dark-haired man who had bumped into Maggie Dimond on the Tupelov's aisle was now leaning idly against a wall, smoking a cigarette. He looked like any other traveller waiting on baggage coming through.

But the last time Gaunt had seen him, the same man had been close to the tail end of the queue of passengers lining up at the start of the immigration checks.

How had he done it, how could he have done it? For a moment, their eyes met across the hall. The man considered him with casual, bored disinterest for a moment, then yawned.

"I'm in glassware—scientific equipment," said Alford breezily. "For me, it's a buying trip. The Czechs are among the best in glass, and desperate for foreign currency. Put that together and if you're from the West you can't lose."

Gaunt hardly heard him. The dark-haired man had eased away from where he'd been standing and was moving unhurriedly across the baggage hall. Maggie Dimond had just come through the last of the control desks. She took a few steps, paused, looked around as if seeking a porter, then shrugged and stayed where she was, her attention fixed on the baggage point. The dark-haired man slowed, stopped about ten feet away from her, and lit another cigarette.

"What's your line, Gaunt?" asked Alford. He sounded puzzled, as if he felt ignored. "Industry, or—?"

"Me?" Gaunt shook his head vaguely. "Nothing special. I'm finding out what's on offer."

Alford gave up for the moment and turned away.

Across the hall, Maggie Dimond took another few paces nearer the baggage pick-up. The man watching her drifted in the same direction, stopping when she stopped, leaving the same gap as before.

Tight-lipped, Gaunt waited. Add the break-in at the widow's cottage, the break-in she hadn't bothered to report, and a surprising number of people seemed to have an interest in where Maggie Dimond went and what she did.

But he could think of only one kind of authority that could get anyone through the Czech arrival procedures so quickly. The Czechs wanted to know more about Maggie Dimond, wanted to know badly enough to place one of their people on the flight out from London. Which would mean the man was OBZ—Czech intelligence—who learned most of their methods at the KGB school.

He left the thought there as the baggage began arriving. Going forward with Carol, he placed himself close to Maggie Dimond.

It was inevitable that the dark-haired man's luggage, a small leather grip, was almost first to appear. Carol's suitcase was close behind and Gaunt lifted it clear, then saw Maggie Dimond's two red suitcases arrive.

She stooped, lifted one, and turned for the other. Somehow, the dark-haired man got beside her. He spoke, grinned, and gripped her second suitcase by the handle. Maggie Dimond didn't seem to move, but the sharp heel of her right shoe came down hard on the stranger's instep. He gave a startled grunt of pain, his eyes widened, and he let go. She collected the case, picked up the other, and, ignoring him, started for the customs exit.

Cold fury in his eyes, the stranger hesitated, then limped slowly in the same direction.

"I'll bet that hurt," murmured Carol Marek. She gave Gaunt a quizzical glance. "You saw?"

He nodded, wondering if the widow had just done the next best thing to springing a bear-trap.

"I thought you might," mused Carol.

He raised an eyebrow.

"I've noticed your interest," said Carol acidly. "But she's probably older than you think—and she looks like she would eat you for breakfast."

Getting through customs was another slow chore. More uniformed men, all with spotless white gloves, made a slow examination of the pieces of luggage coming through. He lost sight of Maggie Dimond in the process, heard Carol talking briskly in Czech to the customs man at the next table, and wasn't particularly surprised when she was allowed on with her case unopened.

They left together. A short walk across the main terminal hall, under more flags and banners, took them out of the building. The wind seemed colder than ever, cold enough for snow, and they moved briskly through a bustle of departing vehicles to reach a small blue bus which had *Hotel Smetana* on its sides in large white letters.

After leaving their luggage with the driver, who was loading cases into the rear hatch, they got aboard. Most of the seats were already filled, the Alfords near the back and Maggie Dimond sitting by herself about midway down. But there was no sign of the dark-haired man.

"You're in luck," murmured Carol maliciously, pointing. The seats across the aisle from Maggie Dimond were still vacant. "Come on."

Gaunt had no option but to follow. Carol reached the vacant seats, took the one on the window side, and grinned as he joined her. Then, the moment he had settled, she leaned in front of him, reached across the narrow aisle, and touched Maggie Dimond on the arm.

"Is everything all right?" she asked with a masterly display of concern. "I mean, when you were collecting your baggage—"

"That?" Maggie Dimond looked surprised, then amused. She had a pleasant, slightly husky voice and a precise way of pronouncing every word. "Call it pest control. I don't like airport pick-ups—or having my bottom patted."

"I think he got the message," said Carol. She chuckled. "It looked that way. He'll certainly remember you." She paused and indicated Gaunt. "We're over for the Trade Fair. You too?"

"No." Maggie Dimond gave a tolerant smile. "Just a few days' holiday, exploring around Prague. It's an interesting city, with a lot of history—and history is my hobby." She spared Gaunt a glance. "You're both from Scotland?"

Gaunt nodded.

"I wondered." She turned her attention back to Carol, the smile still there but quizzical. "I thought I saw you with someone else on the flight from Glasgow."

"My boss," said Carol, unperturbed. "He did a hand-over in London—he's the worrying kind." She leaned further forward, her firm body pressing against Gaunt in the process. "I'm Carol Marek, he's Jonathan Gaunt. Hello."

"I—I'm Margaret Dimond." The woman's manner became suddenly withdrawn and she hesitated, as if looking for a way out of the conversation. "Don't expect to see much of me. I'll be out and about a lot."

"It will be that way for most of us," agreed Gaunt.

Another group of passengers had pushed their way onto the bus and a large man carrying an Aeroflot flight bag was heading for the spare seat. "Still, how about having a drink with us this evening. Carol knows Prague well—maybe she can help you plan things."

Maggie Dimond gave a reluctant nod, then the man with the Aeroflot bag slumped down beside her, ending the matter. A moment later the bus door closed, the engine rumbled to life, and the vehicle began moving with much grating of gears. As it weaved a slow way clear of the airport's arrival and departure traffic, Gaunt felt a nudge against his ribs.

"What's your interest?" demanded Carol Marek softly. She thumbed discreetly across the aisle. "In her, I mean. Do I get to know?"

"Anything wrong in being friendly?" asked Gaunt. He saw the puzzled suspicion in her brown eyes, the way her lips formed a firm, determined line, and sighed. "What's on your mind?"

"That she's either one hyperneurotic female, or a liar—like you," muttered Carol, frowning. "That character she crippled at the airport didn't look the bottom-patting type. It was something else, wasn't it?"

Gaunt shrugged. "How should I know?"

"That's what I'm trying to find out," said the girl. "What's special about her?"

"Nothing," lied Gaunt patiently. He let a sway of the bus bring them closer. "And you're the one who started talking to her. Your turn—why?"

"To see what would happen," admitted Carol. "I wondered about her, that's all." She paused. "You?"

"The same, more or less," said Gaunt. He took a coin from his pocket, tossed it, and caught it. "Heads or tails?"

She blinked. "Why?"

"To see whose expense account pays for dinner tonight," he suggested.

She nodded, called tails, and lost. Satisfied, Gaunt tucked the coin away. He wanted the dark-haired girl's company, without being totally certain why. But it made things oddly pleasant that Eric Garfield's company would be footing the bill—and his one hope was that Maggie Dimond wouldn't launch off on anything too quickly.

The Leninova road from Ruzyně airport into Prague runs straight most of the way, but with enough jarring, unfilled pot-holes to make sure no traveller runs the risk of falling asleep.

And it is usually busy. The hotel bus growled along as part of a steady flow of traffic. Trucks and tanker lorries kept up a relentless battle for position, harassed by small, noisy, and often dilapidated cars and motor cycles. Most of the cars were locally made Skodas, any that were West European make had either C.D. or tourist plates, but all gave way without question to the occasional big black Tatra limousine which glided along with curtained windows and uniformed chauffeur. Socialist democracy, like it or not, knew its pecking order.

For the first few kilometres the Leninova road ran through open countryside. Here and there, large dark hares raced away from the verge, seeking fresh cover. Tractors worked in the fields, most of them followed by a squad of women who were planting as they ploughed. The sky was overcast, the sun only breaking through occasionally, and the land looked cold and still, barely wakened from winter.

Then the houses began. Most were drab, modern high-rise apartment blocks, devoid of character or colour. On every level, each main window that faced the street had a small metal flag-pole bracket as a standard fitment. Many, but still a minority, had small versions of the inevitably twinned Russian and Czech flags on display.

Gaunt wondered about the ones that didn't. But the bus passed that area, reached an older part where there were small houses with pink-tiled roofs and tiny gardens. In the midde was an open square and a large four-storey building hung with red banners. Two soldiers with rifles stood sentry at the main door. Not far away, an army truck was stopped at the kerb. The tail-gate was down, the rear canvas screens were open, and several armed soldiers were climbing aboard.

He gave Carol an inquiring glance. She shrugged, then brushed back a stray lock of her dark hair.

"You'll get used to it," she said unemotionally. "Don't worry about that kind—they're Czech militia. They're the ones with the old trucks and the second-hand equipment. The Russians"—she pursed her lips for a moment—"usually they keep a low profile. When they're on the move, it can mean trouble."

The bus grumbled on, still jolting on the occasional pot-hole, travelling in through the suburbs of Prague. Any kind of public building that might matter seemed to have at least one armed militiaman patrolling outside, a lonely figure in long, heavy greatcoat and fur hat . . . and always under the twinned flags and red banners.

There were plenty of other indications that he was no longer in the West. The only advertising billboards shouted political slogans. Where there were shops, they either were closed or had almost bare display windows, and the few people moving in the streets plodded past them without a glance, muffled against the cold.

They reached the start of tramway rails, overtook a long red and cream trolley-car and trailer, then topped a rise. Carol nudged him and smiled.

Prague was spread out below them, a sprawling, beautiful city of tall spires and gabled roof-tops, of broad streets and wooded hills. Through the middle of it all threaded the wide silver ribbon of the River Vltava, barge traffic moving under its ornate bridges, a low mist still clinging here and there in wisping patches. The effect was an image of almost fairy-tale fascination.

"Like it?" asked Carol.

"Yes." He smiled at her obvious enthusiasm.

"My father still says there's not another city quite the same." Her face clouded slightly as the memory sparked another. "I've got to take some postcards back with me. That's the nearest he'll ever get to seeing it again."

Rattling down the hill, the road snaking and twisting, the bus gathered speed, narrowly missed another trolley-car, exchanged horn-blast insults with a couple of taxis, then shuddered to a halt at traffic lights at the bottom. They crossed a bridge over the Vltava at a sedate pace, turned into a square where every lamppost had flags and a loudspeaker installation, then came to a stop outside the Smetana Hotel.

Big and modern, a twelve-storey block that filled one side of the square, the Smetana obviously catered to the capitalist trade. A smiling doorman was dressed in gold-braided Hussar uniform. The lobby area had deep carpets, a fountain, a profusion of potted greenery, and a squad of desk clerks who spoke English with a mid-Atlantic accent.

Most of the new arrivals were allocated rooms on the eighth floor. Gaunt was close enough to Maggie Dimond's elbow to hear her given the key to 817, with Carol next to her. His own room was 806, and by the time he registered both Carol and the widow had gone. He shared an elevator with the Alfords, who were also bound for the eighth floor, at the other end, and a porter showed him his room.

It was large, comfortable, with private bathroom, a refrigerator bar beside the double bed, and a veranda window which looked out towards the river.

He had been travelling long enough for his back to be hurting.

He raided the bar for a can of beer and used it to wash down one of the pain-killer tablets, then flopped on the bed with a sigh of relief.

Closing his eyes, he let his body relax. His mind couldn't.

Something was happening. Something they hadn't reckoned on at the Remembrancer's Office. The dark-haired man at the airport might have vanished, but someone else could have taken over, could be in the hotel now.

That was the puzzle. Unless every instinct he possessed was wrong, some brand of Czech government agency was interested in Maggie Dimond. And that could only mean trouble.

Why? Even if they'd been told, the Czechs weren't likely to lose sleep at the idea of a female of the British tax-collecting species faking her personal income returns. They had to have another reason, one that mattered to them, one that had its roots in why Maggie Dimond made her regular trips to Prague—and knew a Swiss merchant banker with shady connections.

Jonathan Gaunt shifted into a more comfortable position, heard the bedsprings give a faint squeak, and swore at life in general, then Henry Falconer in particular. It was bad enough being on the wrong side of the Iron Curtain without having to guess at questions before he could go looking for answers.

It was ten times worse if he was in direct competition with some Czech security branch, or the people behind them who pulled the strings. One wrong move, and the Queen's and Lord Treasurer's Remembrancer could be sending food parcels to Prague jail for a long time to come. With Henry Falconer moaning about the cost of postage.

A knock on the room door got him to his feet again. When he opened the door, a hotel porter delivered his travel bag and was followed in by a maid with a supply of fresh towels over one arm.

Once he'd got rid of them, Gaunt unpacked. The pain-killer tablet had had time to work and he decided to have a shower. The needle-fine jets of water washed away the last of his travel fatigue and, padding naked out of the bathroom, he lit a cigarette. Then, as he reached for a clean shirt, he stopped.

An envelope had been pushed under his door. It was small, plain, cheap quality, and his name was scribbled in ink on the front. He opened it. The small slip of paper inside carried a brief message in the same handwriting.

"They serve good coffee in the lobby cafeteria. Try it."

Whatever it meant, he had nothing to lose. Gaunt pulled on the clean shirt and finished dressing. As an afterthought, he flushed paper and envelope down the toilet bowl in the bathroom. Then, whistling tunelessly through his teeth, he stubbed his cigarette and left.

He shared an elevator down to the ground floor with a trio of camera-hung Japanese who had Trade Fair badges pinned to their jacket lapels. They left the hotel and boarded a taxi while Gaunt began ambling along inspecting the lobby area. He spent about five minutes glancing at the display cases filled with crystal and leather goods labeled on sale for foreign currency at the state duty-free Tuzex shops, changed some British pounds for *koruny* at the cashier's desk, then located the cafeteria and went in.

There was a choice of counter or table service. He chose a vacant stool at the counter, ordered coffee from a waitress, and sat sipping it slowly.

The cafeteria was moderately busy. It was easy to spot some of the customers as hotel guests, others as well-heeled locals, and some of the remainder as day-shift prostitutes. They were the ones who sat two or three to a table, each little group with its smoothly dressed male minder hovering close.

One girl, young, with dyed blond hair and quick bright eyes, rose after a moment and came up to the counter. She gave a quick, professional smile and moistened her lips with the tip of her tongue.

"Goodbye," said Gaunt mildly.

She blinked, gave a slight shrug, and went back to her table. As she sat down again, she muttered to her companions, thumbed in Gaunt's direction, and they laughed.

"I think she was suggesting their boy-friend should have a try," said an amused, heavily accented voice at his elbow.

Gaunt took another sip of coffee, then glanced round. The middle-aged man who had taken the stool next to him wore a belted leather jacket, jeans, and a heavy roll-neck sweater. Grey-haired, chubby, medium height, he wore spectacles and needed a shave. Giving Gaunt a friendly nod, he ignored him for a moment, rapping on the counter with a coin and ordering a beer.

"Thanks for coming, Mr. Gaunt," he added softly as the waitress turned away. "Tell me, are you important?"

"No," said Gaunt flatly. "Not as far as I know."

"Your people in Edinburgh seem to think differently," murmured the man. He winked. "Janos Barta—you know the name?"

Gaunt stared at him. Janos Barta was the contact name he'd been given, the contact to be used only if he hit trouble.

"Maybe." He waited as the man's beer arrived and Barta paid for it. "Who sent you?"

"Nobody." Barta took a gulp from his drink, let a smile of contentment cross his broad face, then wiped a trace of froth from his lips. "I mean, no one told me to come. But I got a message that you were arriving, that I might hear from you." His voice was a soft murmur. Behind the spectacles, his eyes made another casual inspection of the cafeteria. "I drive a taxi. It is well known to the police that all taxi-drivers are petty capitalist vermin—useful, but vermin. Right now I am trying to sell you the idea of letting me take you sightseeing around Prague. Agreed?"

Gaunt nodded. "Give me a name—one I'll know."

Barta chuckled approvingly. "There is a man called Falconer. I don't know who he is. But he knows your Queen."

"Works for her," corrected Gaunt. "All right, why come here?"

"For my own sake." Barta shrugged. "There is more risk than there used to be. Our neighbours the Poles—what they did might be contagious, so there is more suspicion. Even our own police, who often look the other way, are less tolerant. I want no thick-headed Englishman—"

"Scot," corrected Gaunt. "We like to think there's a difference."

"Not to me," said Barta. "Not if you cause me problems."

Gaunt's mouth tightened. "Then why the hell did you bother to come?"

"Easy, Mr. Gaunt," soothed Barta.

Looking past him, the Czech paused and grinned. Gaunt followed his gaze. The young prostitute with the dyed blond hair had connected. So had the dark-haired girl who had been with her. They were leaving, arm in arm, with two more of the Japanese.

"Advice for tourists." Still grinning, Barta took off his spectacles and rubbed them with a paper napkin. "The ladies come expensive, and they always know today's exchange rates. The going rate is about one hundred and twenty American dollars."

"Inflation hits us all," said Gaunt.

"True." Barta replaced his spectacles. "But in a way I'm like them. You rent me, you don't buy outright. We can do business, but there are limits."

Gaunt nodded.

"Good." Barta relaxed on his stool, took a long gulp of beer, then wiped his lips. "Don't use the contact address—there have been one or two small difficulties at it lately. Just tell your hotel doorman—whoever is on duty—that you want Barta's taxi. Then wait."

"You've an arrangement?"

"On a more general basis." The heavily accented voice held a slight embarrassment. "I have a certain reputation. If a foreigner wants something, and can pay for it—"

"Black market?" asked Gaunt bluntly.

"Not black," protested Barta. "The word is 'grey.'" He took another glance around the crowded cafeteria, as if expecting something to happen, then sighed. "My friend, you are visiting a two-layer economy. More than that—a two-layer nation. The top layer is communist, thin, kept firmly in place by Mother Russia. We accept it's there, most of us, for survival."

"But underneath?"

"We're Czechs. We've been doing it for centuries." Barta winked. "We run one hell of a little capitalist society and try not to get caught. Now—what do you want?"

Gaunt had been trying to make up his mind about that. Now he decided.

"A woman arrived with me on the airport bus. Margaret Dimond —mid-forties, well-built—"

Barta stopped him. "I can get the rest."

"Right." Gaunt considered the man for a moment. Several things about Barta intrigued him. They would have to wait. "She'll be moving about. I'll be near her when I can, but—"

"You want cover the rest of the time." Barta sucked his lips then nodded. "It should be possible. Not easy—possible."

"You'd better know," said Gaunt slowly. "Other people could be interested in her."

"I see." Barta left it there for a moment as their waitress returned, mopping her way along the counter-top with a damp cloth. He smiled at her, then, once she'd passed, he drew a deep, resigned breath. "This woman—is she political?"

"No. At least, I don't think so."

"You're not certain?" Barta gave him a deliberate grin, still acting the taxi-driver trying to make a deal, but his words came in an angry whisper. "In this country, there's one hell of a difference, Mr. Gaunt."

"But you'll do it?"

Barta hesitated. Once again he took another, apparently casual glance around. Then, suddenly, he relaxed.

"Young fool," he said softly. "Still—"

He didn't finish. There was a sudden, brief scuffle among the tables at the far end of the cafeteria. A chair overturned. As conversation froze to a total silence, a thin, pale-faced young man was dragged rapidly towards the exit by two others. The young man looked frightened. His companions, burly, casually dressed men, moved with assurance.

They vanished. The whole cafeteria seemed to sigh. Someone gave a forced laugh. Then the buzz of conversation resumed.

"Some never learn," said Barta quietly. He shrugged. "Small fry, Mr. Gaunt—I've seen him around. There are plenty like him, illegal money-changers. They'll give a tourist twice the official rate, three times if you hold out."

"Then sell at a profit?"

Barta nodded. "But sometimes they pick the wrong customer, in the wrong place. I had these two spotted as police, and for a moment I thought—" He dismissed the rest with a head-shake. "To your problem. I'll do what I can. If it becomes dangerous, I say goodbye."

"That's all I ask," said Gaunt.

"That's all you'll get." Barta grinned, finished his beer, and laid down the glass. "If you get word I'm looking for you, try the Old Town Square."

"Tell me something," said Gaunt quietly, "how long have you been driving taxis?"

"Long enough," said Barta flatly. He saw the question in Gaunt's eyes and shrugged. "Before that? Once, I taught philosophy at Prague University. But the wrong kind. We all make mistakes, eh?"

He didn't wait for an answer. Placing some loose change on the counter to pay for his drink, he made to rise. Then, suddenly, he sat down again.

"That young fool who was arrested," he said softly, "I've just seen why. A tall man, wearing a Trade Fair badge. Make it casual."

Gaunt brought out his cigarettes and glanced towards the corner tables as he lit one. The man was well-dressed, with strong, handsome features and close-cropped, prematurely grey hair.

"Got him."

"His name is Brozman," said Barta. "Colonel Anatole Brozman—"

"OBZ?"

"In his time." Barta sucked his teeth. "Maybe he still is—who can be sure? But at the moment he runs a very efficient section in Prague area STB—internal security. Initials change—people don't." He eyed Gaunt through his spectacles. "One benefit of my past connections is I know Brozman, though hopefully he doesn't know I exist—or care. But he's nobody's fool. If he's interested in your lady—"

Gaunt shook his head. "I haven't said that."

Barta gave a cynical grimace. "If he is, my advice would be forget about her and go sightseeing. You'd have a much happier time."

Slipping down from his stool, Barta pulled on an old leather hat and ambled away. Gaunt watched him go out then took another glance towards the table in the corner.

His mouth tightened. Someone else had just joined Colonel Brozman. OBZ or STB—Janos Barta had been right, initials were incidental.

The dark-haired man from the London flight was now in the chair opposite Brozman, talking earnestly.

Gaunt signalled the waitress. He shook his head as she reached for the coffee-pot.

At that moment, a brandy seemed better.

CHAPTER 3

Jonathan Gaunt waited another ten minutes in the cafeteria, then left. More arrivals were checking in at the reception desk as he went through the hotel lobby, and he had to squeeze aboard the elevator which took him up to the eighth floor, sharing it with a Dutch couple and their luggage, one of the hotel porters, and three stout, well-dressed men who spoke German and wore Rotary Club badges.

At the eighth floor, he got out and deliberately walked along to Maggie Dimond's room. A multilingual "Do Not Disturb" sign had been hung on the door handle. Happy to leave it that way, he went to Carol Marek's door, knocked, and waited.

It opened after a moment and she looked out.

"Hello." She opened the door wider and beckoned him in. "I'm not ready for social calls, but come in."

He did. As the door closed again, he realized Carol was wearing a white robe and almost certainly nothing else. In her bare feet, her dark hair pinned back, she looked very much smaller, younger, and more vulnerable.

"Bath time—just about, anyway." She nodded apologetically towards the litter of unpacked clothes which covered most of her bed and spread from there to the chairs. "Welcome to my shambles." Moving as spoke, she gathered a handful of folded underwear from one chair and dumped it on the bed. "Sit down, Jonny. No, hell—wait."

He grinned as she rescued an overlooked pair of tights.

"What time do we meet for that drink?" he asked.

"That free drink," she corrected cheerfully. "There's a Ministry of Trade reception for our kind of people downstairs at seven, walk-in style."

"Fine." He thumbed in the direction of Maggie Dimond's room. "What about—"

"I thought you'd ask," said Carol. "She told me it was happening. The hotel switchboard called the wrong room with the message. I've invited her along." Seeing Gaunt wasn't going to use the chair, she sat in it clasping her hands round her knees. The robe parted alarmingly in the process. "Any other problems?"

"No." He walked over to her window. The view was down towards the square outside the hotel. But he also noticed the small balcony which she shared with Maggie Dimond, divided by a low, decorative iron railing. "How about your relatives here, the ones you told me about? Planning on visiting them?"

"I'm not sure." Carol frowned and shook her head slowly. "Probably not. They live a long way out." She paused. "Jonny—"

"Yes?" He turned from the window.

"She was asking about you—the merry widow, I mean." She frowned at his expression. "I'm serious. Who you were, what you did—she worked at it. Casually enough, but determined to find out."

"And?" asked Gaunt.

"I told her you're a friend of my boss and you work with a Government exhibition committee—that's all." Carol noticed how the robe was gaping and pulled it together again. "She seemed happy enough with that. But she left me wondering."

"About what?" asked Gaunt.

"Whether it's true." She considered him pointedly.

"Why shouldn't it be?"

She shrugged. "Just a feeling I have."

"The dreaded woman's intuition?" Gaunt rubbed his chin. "You mean you don't always rely on computer print-outs?"

"No, I don't." She sighed and got to her feet. "Look, I treated myself to a bottle of stupidly expensive bath-oil for this trip. The sooner you've gone—"

Gaunt took the hint and left.

Heading for his room, he met the plump, bustling figure of John Alford striding towards the elevator with his wife trailing behind him. The Midlands glass buyer beamed a quick greeting.

"Know about the free drinks?" he asked, and winked. "Lubrication for the wheels of commerce—nothing like it, eh?"

"A sales invoice in every bottle," said Gaunt. "You're going?"

"The last time I turned down a free drink, they sent for a doctor," said Alford. He dug his wife in the ribs. "Thought I was ill, didn't they?"

She gave her usual weary, dutiful nod.

"You were," she said sadly. "Pneumonia. He nearly died, Mr. Gaunt. But he got better instead."

They went on towards the elevator.

Once in his room, Gaunt switched on the TV set and watched the black-and-white picture. It was a children's cartoon programme, the adventures of two rabbits trying to avoid being trapped in a cage.

Lounging on the bed, Gaunt watched it abstractedly. The Czechs were experts in animation. Their cartoon films had always been reckoned the best in Europe. The best, with a delicate, built-in ability to weave a strand of gentle, sometimes sad but always endearing optimism into slapstick plot.

The rabbits pranced across the TV screen, being chased again. He watched them gloomily.

Substitute people for rabbits and the plot came too close to home. He might have come out to Prague in something similar to the role of hunter, but was that going to last?

Already Carol Marek had her suspicions, though he had hardly begun. For that he had only himself to blame. On the credit side there was Barta. The onetime university lecturer turned taxi-driver would be a useful ally if he stayed around. But the real factor, the unknown factor, was why a Czech security force colonel was so interested in the Hotel Smetana.

The reason had to be Maggie Dimond. The widow from Inland Revenue was trouble, more trouble than he'd ever imagined likely.

The cartoon ended. The next programme feature began, a jolly, all-action comedy about life with the happy members of a Comicon country's crack tank battalion.

Gaunt decided he'd preferred the rabbits.

Carol Marek had suggested seven-thirty. When Gaunt knocked on her room door, she emerged wearing a powder-blue cocktail dress which was simple in style and cut and totally feminine. She had high-heeled sandals and carried a small black evening bag. Apart from the gold chain at her throat, her only jewellery was a slim gold bracelet watch and a pair of tiny amethyst stud earrings.

"You look good," Gaunt told her, meaning it.

"I should," she said gravely. "The damned dress cost me the best part of two weeks' pay." Then she grinned. "So let's put it to work."

They took an elevator down to the ground floor. The Trade Fair reception was in the hotel's Crystal Room, along a corridor to the right, and other guests were drifting in the same direction. A girl on reception duty at the door asked their names but didn't ask for credentials. They were handed thick folders filled with Trade Fair public relations material, then waved through.

The Crystal Room was big, with a high, ornately painted ceiling, crystal chandelier lighting, and long red-velvet window drapes. About a hundred people were talking and moving around under the glittering lights, their voices a babble of languages punctuated by laughter. A waitress offered them glasses of a sweet white wine.

"I seem to get a message," murmured Carol. She sipped her drink. "Comrade capitalists, we want your business."

Gaunt shrugged. He never felt at ease in a cocktail party scene, but the women among the guests were expensively dressed, the men smoothly tailored. There wasn't a uniform or political banner in sight. The same scene could have been London, Paris, or New York apart from the harsh Balkan tang of the cigarette smoke hanging in the air.

"Export first, worry about the politics afterwards," he said stonily. "We do the same sometimes, don't we?"

He could see the plump figure of John Alford half-way across the room. Round face flushed and beaming, he was in the middle of a group, talking earnestly. His wife was beside him, wearing something that looked like a sack covered in sequins. But Gaunt was more interested in locating Maggie Dimond.

"Over there," said Carol a moment later. She indicated another group, standing under one of the crystal chandeliers. "Just behind them."

He nodded, spotting the distinctive, coppery hair, and they eased their way towards her. She was talking to someone, but the group in front blocked Gaunt's view until he'd almost reached her. Then, as she saw them and gave a slight smile of a greeting, the tall, grey-haired man with her turned. Gaunt had to stifle a grunt of surprise as Colonel Anatole Brozman eyed them with a polite curiosity.

"Two friends I met on the flight," said Maggie Dimond. She

switched the same slight smile to Brozman. "Colonel, I told you I was gatecrashing. But you can be nice to them—they're Trade Fair people."

Brozman chuckled and ran a hand along his chin. Most of his attention stayed with Maggie Dimond. She was in a bottle-green silk dress, close-fitting and with a deep, eye-catching plunge of neckline.

"Your credentials satisfy me, Mrs. Dimond," he said firmly. He had a soft voice, almost lazy, and a grin that showed strong white teeth as Maggie Dimond made the introductions and he shook hands with Carol and Gaunt. "Enjoying our party? I can promise you won't see an order book till tomorrow."

"What about you, Colonel?" asked Gaunt. "What do you sell? Soldiers?"

Unruffled, Brozman shook his head. "I'm attached to our Foreign Office. My role is—ah—to be available. To take care of problems." Deliberately, he turned to Carol. "Mrs. Dimond tells me you speak Czech. Few foreigners do—we have to learn their languages instead. But Marek—?"

"My father," said Carol shortly.

Brozman nodded slowly. "Interesting. But you're from Scotland. Did you know that centuries ago a Scottish princess came to Prague as our queen?"

Carol gave an uncertain frown.

"He's right." Maggie Dimond gave a crisp nod of agreement. "Her name was Elizabeth." Hardly pausing, she went on, "Daughter of James the Sixth of Scotland, married Frederick the Fifth who was elected king of Bohemia in 1619—"

"Unfortunately he lasted less than a year," murmured Brozman. "We call him the Winter King. There was a war, and his army was defeated on the White Mountain, not far from here." He considered Maggie Dimond with undisguised curiosity. "You know our history?"

"I read some books."

She left it at that, in a way that seemed almost deliberate. Gaunt remembered the entry in her file, the one which said Maggie Dimond had been an Honours history graduate before she'd joined the happy ranks of Inland Revenue. But Brozman seemed satisfied.

"I can try to find you more," he said mildly, then stopped and frowned across the room, which was still filling. "There's someone I have to talk with—a Belgian. He has visa troubles. Excuse me."

He left them, weaving an unhurried, confident way through the chattering guests, then disappeared.

Carol and Maggie Dimond began talking. Half-listening to them, Gaunt nodded now and again and made appropriate noises. But he was thinking about Brozman. Janos Barta had claimed Brozman was an STB officer. All right, Barta could have been lying, building up his own importance. Yet that was unlikely. In which case Brozman was an unorthodox operator—and they could be the most dangerous of all.

But exactly what the hell was going on?

Suddenly he realized Maggie Dimond had spoken to him, was waiting for an answer.

"Sorry." He grimaced an apology. "I missed that."

"I asked which government department you work for," said Maggie Dimond again. "Carol told me about the exhibition committee, the reason you're here."

"Development Research—we're a small unit." Gaunt knew it existed and was safe. "We're part of Trade and Industry—at least, we're on their budget." A waitress appeared at his elbow, offering more of the white wine, and he took a fresh glass. "What about you, Mrs. Dimond?"

"Work?" Her manner cooled a degree or two. "An office job, the kind I try to forget when I'm away from it."

"It's a sensible policy." She'd blocked the question neatly, but while he had the chance he took it. "What about while you're here? Made any firm plans yet?"

"No." A blend of caution and annoyance entered her attitude. Then she seemed to feel some kind of answer was necessary. "I may stay within the city, I may hire a car and explore further out."

"There's plenty to see," mused Carol. "Prague's called the city of a hundred spires. You can begin in the tenth century and go on from there."

"Romanesque through Gothic to Baroque." Maggie Dimond nodded almost curtly and glanced deliberately at her wrist-watch. "There are supposed to be State Tourist Board people among this crowd—they helped me last time. I think I'll try and find them before dinner."

She gave a brief glimmer of a farewell smile and left before either of them could answer.

"And goodbye to you," said Carol, as the older woman disappeared, lost somewhere behind a noisy group of Arabs. "Did you feel the chill?"

Gaunt shrugged then stifled a groan. John Alford and his wife were ploughing a way towards them.

"I've something to tell you, young fellow," said Alford expansively as he reached them. "Something about this hotel, right?" He barely paused for breath. "We got it from that Czech colonel in the Foreign Office, didn't we, Helen?"

She nodded dutifully. Gaunt wondered at the optimism of parents who'd given her the name of a beauty who'd launched a thousand ships. Dumpy, earnest, Alford's wife didn't look as though she'd have influenced a canal barge.

"It's the rooms," said Alford. "I asked him straight, was our room bugged—you know, a microphone, anything like that." He paused and spluttered. "He just smiled, said he'd check the tapes in the morning and tell me!"

"I think our Colonel Brozman has a warped sense of humour," said Gaunt.

"But you can't be sure, right?" countered Alford.

It was fifteen minutes before they managed to escape from the couple, Carol making the categoric statement she had to find the powder room. By then, the Crystal Room reception was beginning to wind down and a first trickle of people were leaving.

"I'm hungry," said Carol.

"And you're paying," reminded Gaunt.

"Chivalry, R.I.P.," she agreed. "But I get to keep the receipt."

The Hotel Smetana had two restaurants, and she chose the more expensive, located on the top floor and billed as the Observation Martinu. The elevator which took them up opened on a candle-lit area with tables ranged around full-length windows. Two violinists in gypsy costume played music with origins long before either world war, and waiters in white jackets bustled with trays.

Their table looked south. The night sky was clear and the moon shone down on a city which seemed an endless expanse of spires and domes and sparkling lights. Reality might be different, but it was hidden and for the moment Gaunt was happy for it to stay that way.

Carol Marek seemed to feel the same. They ordered, talked a little over a drink, then ate. He'd let Carol choose for them both, and they had *Prazska sunka,* a morsel of smoked, thin-sliced ham, as a starter, followed by a clear chicken soup. *Vareny kapr,* boiled carp with butter sauce, was the lowest-priced main course, but as delicate in texture as it was appetizing.

Gaunt shook his head at the idea of a sweet and they asked the waiter for coffee.

"My thanks to Trellux Components," said Gaunt gravely. Carol had taken a pack of slim cheroots from her handbag and he lit one for her, then took one of his own cigarettes. The gypsy fiddlers were doing another circuit of the restaurant, coming near their table. "What happened to the Comicon food shortage?"

"It's real." Carol toyed with the cheroot, her lips tightening for a moment. "Get out on the streets early enough, and you'll see the shop queues. In here, it's window dressing—and hard currency." She stopped, smiled at the fiddle players, then looked around the other tables. "Your favourite lady hasn't shown up."

Gaunt shrugged. There was the other restaurant, other possible reasons, and he'd already lost what little enthusiasm he'd had for the case of Maggie Dimond and her tax evasion. Any time he thought about it, he felt like a man who'd stepped on a puddle and found there was no bottom.

"What's she done?" asked Carol bluntly.

"Since we got here?" Gaunt shook his head. "Nothing."

"I know that, damn you," she said. "And you know what I'm asking."

Gaunt sighed. "Carol—"

"No, Jonny, forget it." She cut him short. "You're right and I'm sorry. It's none of my damned business. Don't worry, I won't spook her."

"Maybe I should tell you some of it." Gaunt forestalled the objection he saw coming. "There's a reason, a good one." He leaned his elbows on the table between them, knowing he wanted to talk. "Yes, I'm here to keep an eye on Maggie Dimond. Back home she works for Inland Revenue—whatever she says. But she's also in deep personal tax trouble."

She stared at him in something close to disbelief. "She gets chased across Europe just because she's a naughty taxperson?"

"Naughty in a big way," emphasized Gaunt. "Look, when Inland Revenue find they're being conned by one of their own people, they go berserk—that sort of thing rates as a cardinal sin. It also happens there's a hell of a lot of money involved, money that could be coming from this country."

"How?"

He shook his head. "We don't know."

"But you want to find out." She sighed. "Why you?"

"Because I work in something called the Remembrancer's Department. If a situation is awkward, or other people want rid of it, we sort things out." He paused, aware of how attractive she looked in the candle-light, uncertain if he should go on. But on balance it might be better if she knew the rest. "Part of the mess is that it looks as though the Czechs are interested in her."

"I see," she said slowly, soberly. "Thanks for the warning." Then she surprised him again. "Would part of it be the colonel we met in the Crystal Room?"

"Perhaps."

"And the man at the airport?"

He nodded.

"Then your tax lady really has problems." Her lips pursed for a moment. "From anything I've heard, Czech security can make the KGB look like gentlemen. Maybe you should stay clear of her—well clear."

"I've had that notion," he admitted.

Their waiter came over, bringing coffee and brandy. Carol talked to him in Czech and he grinned as he answered, shaking his head. Then he went away.

"What was that about?" asked Gaunt.

"Idle chat." She stubbed what was left of her cheroot then raised her brandy glass in a mock toast. "To your tax lady. I've a boss who's luckier than he knows. Eric Garfield is probably worrying about the kind of job I'll do for his beloved Trellux. If he knew about this, he'd have kittens on the spot."

Gaunt smiled. Knowing Garfield, it was a reasonable possibility.

"Originally, he would have been here too." Carol gave a mock grimace at the notion. "But that was before his wife announced she was pregnant."

"She's—" Gaunt stared at her, all thoughts of Maggie Dimond wiped from his mind.

"Pregnant," repeated Carol patiently. "They're both over the moon about it."

"Yes." Gaunt moistened his lips, oddly shaken by the news. "They would be."

Eric Garfield would make a textbook ideal father to any child. But Patti pregnant, carrying Garfield's child . . .

"He probably thought you'd heard." Carol misunderstood his silence. "That's why he wouldn't mention it."

"I suppose so." Gaunt sipped his brandy, then looked out at the lights of the city and called himself a fool. Patti had settled down and was happy. That she and Garfield should have a family was normal, natural, inevitable. But it was still as if an old, fading wound had suddenly begun hurting in a new way. "His wife—how is she?"

"Blooming." Carol gave a soft chuckle. "In every sense of the word. And the way he's galloping about, they're going to have the world's first computer-controlled nursery ready and waiting."

He nodded, saying nothing.

She frowned. "Anything wrong?"

"No." He smiled at her and raised his glass. "To their good news."

The gypsy violin duo disappeared and their place was taken by four middle-aged musicians in dinner jackets who filled a pocket-sized stage and began playing dance music which had its roots in the fifties. A few couples took to the floor.

"I know I'm picking up the tab," said Carol Marek deliberately. "I'm also planning on an early night—for real, because Eric Garfield collected me about dawn this morning." Her fingers tapped on the table in rhythm to the music. "But—"

Gaunt took the hint.

She danced well, considerably better than he could. She also stayed close, humming under her breath. But she broke off with an indignant yelp when he stood on her foot.

The nearest couple, a tall, shaven-headed man and a small, dumpy woman who had to be his wife, smiled. The woman had a set of gold-plated teeth and murmured her sympathy.

"Bloody Russians," said Carol indignantly once they were clear. She glared in the direction of the shaven head, then subsided. "All right, I've still one set of toes intact."

They stayed on the floor a little longer then returned to their table. Carol signalled for the bill, signed it, and added a tip which left their waiter beaming.

She stayed silent in the elevator which took them down to the eighth floor. They went along the corridor to her room and she put her key in the lock, opened the door, then turned to face Gaunt.

"It was a nice evening," she said quietly.

"Yes." He hesitated. "Next time—?"

"You pay." She laughed, and kissed him firmly on the lips. "Good night, Jonny."

She was in her room with the door closed before he could answer.

In a way, Gaunt felt glad to be alone. Patti was still too much on his mind. He drew a deep breath, knowing it was just one more step along their separate ways, one more thing to accept.

He shrugged, glanced casually at Maggie Dimond's room door, and saw the "Do Not Disturb" sign was back on the handle.

Turning, he went along to his own room. He found the bed had been turned down. A chocolate mint wrapped in silver paper had been placed on the pillow, next to a breakfast card.

Gaunt glanced at his wrist-watch. It was still only eleven o'clock. Feeling restless, he went over to the window and looked out at the night. The traffic lights on a bridge over the silvered water of the Vltava blinked and changed to green. A solitary tramcar rumbled across in one direction; two cars came from the other side.

On an impulse, he pulled on his old sheepskin jacket and went out again, determined to walk off some of what was troubling him. He was on his way along the corridor to the elevator when he heard a door open somewhere ahead.

A man came out of Maggie Dimond's room, closed the door quietly behind him, and walked towards the elevator. He was broad-built, bearded, and in his early forties. He had dark, greying hair, an assured air, and wore a yellow anorak jacket with a fur collar over a dark blue suit and black roll-neck sweater.

Gaunt reached the elevator first and pressed the "Down" button. The stranger gave him an unconcerned glance, then ignored him, waiting, lighting a cigarette.

The elevator door opened, they got in, and the stranger pressed the ground floor button. Eyes half-closed, cigarette dangling from his bearded lips, the man leaned against one of the metal walls, then stepped out briskly as the door opened at the Smetana's lobby.

Gaunt held back for a moment, then followed. The stranger crossed the lobby, reached the main exit, and went out into the street. Quickening his pace, Gaunt was almost there when the doors flew open and a torrent of people began pouring in. A bus had stopped outside and the people coming from it wore Trade Fair badges, obviously back from some organized outing.

Cursing, he pushed through the crowd. Two Japanese grinned apologetically as he trampled on their feet. An English group, the women swathed in fur and giggling, their escorts' breath heavy with alcohol, protested as he shoved past them.

Outside at last, he felt his nostrils stung by the chill night air. The man in the yellow jacket had gone, the bus had emptied and was pulling away. The only person in sight was the hotel doorman, stamping his feet against the cold, his hands tucked deep into the pockets of his Hussar uniform.

There was nothing he could do about it. Fastening the sheepskin, Gaunt squared his shoulders and set off at an ambling slouch.

In a minute or so he was in a street which led along the side of the river. He reached the bridge and the traffic lights he'd seen from his window, then stood for a moment while they blinked their automatic sequence to a junction absolutely empty of traffic. Crossing over, he wondered how many other cities in the world had main streets so silent, so empty of life at that hour.

Not totally empty. As he turned away from the river, crossing at another junction, a police car cruised towards him. It had a large blue light on its roof, bold VB lettering on its doors, and two of a crew aboard. He knew they were watching him before the car slowed to a crawl. A hand spotlight clicked on, bathed him briefly in its glare, then clicked off again.

The police car cruised on. The air temperature was still dropping, the cold penetrating through the sheepskin, and he decided to turn back towards the Smetana. He could see the high rise of the hotel building to his left and turned towards it, heading along a narrow, darkened street where iron railings guarded a very small and very old graveyard. The building beyond them was a synagogue, the Star of David above its door just visible in the faint glow from a street light.

Then it happened. First, a muffled cry came from the darkness ahead, followed by the sounds of a short, quick scuffle. A figure came out of the shadows at a staggering run, heading towards him. Two men appeared close behind in purusit.

The staggering figure saw him, lifted an arm as if pleading for help, then was struck down. A knife glinted in the pallid edge of a street lamp's glow.

Shouting, Gaunt sprang forward and the men standing over their victim reacted as if stung. A pistol barked, the bullet ricocheted angrily off the synagogue wall close to Gaunt's head, then they were running. Gaunt reached the fallen man, stopped, heard a car start up.

Headlamps glared. The car roared along the street, stopped with a squeal of brakes, and the two men tumbled aboard. Doors closing, it accelerated again, mounted the pavement, and came straight for Gaunt.

Almost blinded by the glare, Gaunt threw himself back, felt the car brush his clothing, and saw the vehicle give a violent lurch as it went over the injured man's body. It kept moving, tyres screaming as it turned a corner and vanished.

For a moment he had seen the face behind the steering wheel. A broad, flint-hard face with a deep scar on one cheek, the kind of face it was hard to forget. Matthew Garr, who had been Maggie Dimond's escort before she left Scotland, was now in Prague.

The Swiss merchant banker was certainly anything but alone—and ready to kill. But for what purpose?

Bewildered, heart still pounding, Gaunt crossed slowly to the crumpled shape lying face-down in a dark, gradually spreading pool of blood close to the edge of the gutter. As he knelt to touch the man, the quick patter of running feet came from further up the old, ill-lit street.

Gaunt twisted round and could just make out a pale, moving blob among the shadows. Seconds later, a light-weight engine barked to life, then screaming through its gears, a motor cycle raced away.

It passed under a street lamp. The rider, hunched over the handlebars of his small machine, wore a yellow anorak with a wide fur collar. Speed increasing, the machine vanished from sight and the howl of its engine faded.

Tight-lipped, more uncertain than ever, Gaunt turned back to the bleeding, broken figure at his feet. Gently, he eased the injured man over on his side.

The movement brought a low, bubbling moan of pain. Then, for the first time, he saw the man's face.

He was Brozman's dark-haired aide, the OBZ agent on the flight from London. Blood dribbling from his mouth, he was conscious, face twisting in a new agony as he tried to draw breath and move his lips.

"They've gone," said Gaunt quietly. "It's over."

Whatever the man had been doing, whatever he stood for, was secondary. He was dying.

The man managed another painful, bubbling breath which brought fresh blood to his mouth. One hand moved in a spasmodic effort, found Gaunt's arm, and gripped weakly. Then suddenly, his eyes widened and he stared up.

Resignedly, Gaunt turned his head and met the stony gaze of a Czech militiaman. The rifle in the militiaman's hands jabbed against Gaunt's spine in an angry, unspoken order which needed no interpretation.

Slowly, Gaunt eased away from the man on the ground, and backed against the cold brick of the synagogue wall.

There were two militiamen. The second moved in, slung his rifle, and bent low over Brozman's aide, speaking in a low, urgent voice. The dying man's lips moved, the militiaman trying hard to catch what he was struggling to say.

A startled expression crossed the militiaman's face. Opening the man's coat, he reached inside, brought out a wallet, stared at what was in it, then rose quickly. He spoke rapidly to his companion, then hurried off into the darkness.

He was gone only a few minutes, then came trotting back again. Bending over the man on the ground, he shook his head. Then he seemed to remember Gaunt, crossed to his companion, and gestured.

The rifle lowered almost reluctantly, still held ready. Very deliberately, making sure there could be no misunderstanding, Gaunt reached into his jacket and produced his passport. It was examined carefully by each militiaman in turn, then there were nods and it was handed back.

They spoke no English, but one beckoned him to look at the still figure on the ground, shrugging expressively.

Brozman's man was dead.

Gaunt brought out his cigarettes. The militiamen took one each, grinned their thanks, and they shared a light. They were still smoking when two police cars arrived, followed by an ambulance. The police and the militiamen talked, and several curious stares came Gaunt's way, but he was left alone. If any of the rest of Prague's million or so population were anywhere near, they stayed well clear.

Another ten minutes passed, then a large black Tatra limousine growled into the street, headlamps sweeping the scene. The militiamen stiffened, the police immediately began to look busy.

The limousine halted and Colonel Brozman got out of the front passenger seat, bareheaded, fastening a hip-length fur jacket. One of the militiamen stepped forward and saluted. Brozman came towards him, paused for a moment to look down at the dead man, then listened to the ramrod-stiff militiaman's report. When that was finished, he gave a curt nod then came over to Gaunt.

"I hoped to meet you again, Mr. Gaunt," said Brozman almost wearily, "but not like this. My apologies. I need your help." He pursed his lips. "You saw what happened?"

Gaunt nodded. "Some of it." The night chill seemed to have robbed his feet of all feeling, and he shivered.

Brozman noticed and gave a thin, reassuring smile.

"Don't worry. Before the—the victim died, he said you tried to help him." His lips tightened briefly. "Unfortunately, that was all."

"I see." Gaunt found it easy enough to maintain a worried air. "Who was he?"

An odd flicker showed in Brozman's eyes, then had gone. Stuffing his hands into the pockets of his fur jacket, he shook his head.

"We still have to find out," he said flatly. "From his papers, he was a local man, but until we check—" He stopped and shrugged. "Prague still has its reactionary criminal elements, Mr. Gaunt. Don't you have a saying, 'when thieves fall out . . .'?"

Gaunt nodded. If Brozman wanted to lie, it hardly mattered.

"However, at least when the police heard a foreigner was involved, a possible Trade Fair guest, they had sense enough to contact me," added Brozman. "Now tell me what you saw."

"Not much." Gaunt shivered again, fighting against the chill. He had been given time to think and decide and was ready to gamble on the result. "I decided I'd had a drink too many and that a walk would clear my head. When I got here, well"—he gestured towards the dead man—"I saw him being chased by two men. They knocked him down and it looked like they were going to rob him. Then they saw me."

"And?" Brozman raised an eyebrow.

"They changed their minds," said Gaunt simply. "There was a car. They jumped into it, tried to run me down, and drove straight over him. That's all, except there was a driver, of course—so there were three of them."

"Yes." Brozman sucked his teeth. "These men—can you describe any of them?" He sighed as Gaunt shook his head. "Or the car?"

"No. It happened too fast." Gaunt grimaced apologetically. "I was busy getting clear, and the street lighting isn't good."

"Thank you." Brozman didn't hide his disappointment. "Of course, the police will require a statement later."

"Any time." Gaunt shivered again, deliberately. "Mind if I get back to somewhere warmer now?"

"Of course." Brozman nodded, suddenly disinterested. "My apologies again, Mr. Gaunt. Good night."

Gaunt walked away. He looked back only once, when he'd gone some distance. The little section of street beside the old synagogue was bathed in light from the police cars' headlamps. Brozman stood in the middle of it, alone, a stiff, angry figure.

Three minutes later he was back inside the comfort and warmth of the Hotel Smetana. Several guests were still drinking in the ground floor bar and a tall, smartly dressed prostitute with dark hair and a long wolf-skin coat tried to proposition him as he headed for the elevator.

Nothing had changed.

He went up to his room, stripped off his old sheepskin, raided the little bar beside his bed, drank a miniature of brandy straight from the bottle, stood over the nearest radiator, and gradually began to thaw out.

The traffic outside seemed to have grown. It became a steady, heavy rumble that sounded all too familiar from his past and he went over to the window.

The traffic lights on the bridge over the river had been switched off. Blue lamps winking, police cars were stationed at either end and a long stream of military vehicles were passing over it. He saw trucks and personnel carriers crammed with men, support vehicles and armoured scout cars, some medium tanks mounted on transporters, then more personnel carriers.

They had bold red stars on their sides. Carol had told him the Russians kept a low profile.

But they existed. Particularly at night.

He stood there until the last truck had crossed and the traffic lights were once again winking.

Somewhere out there was the man called Matthew Garr. Somewhere out there too was the bearded man with the yellow anorak.

They both knew Maggie Dimond.

So did Colonel Brozman.

He swore, gave up, then remembered what John Alford had said. The plump businessman was a fumbling menace, but was it possible the rooms were bugged?

He checked. It took half an hour and he found nothing, as he'd expected. He undressed and got into bed.

It was some time before he got to sleep, and when he did, he dreamed of Patti.

CHAPTER 4

The swish of curtains being opened and a bright glare of sunlight wakened Jonathan Gaunt late the next morning. He groaned, yawned, and a young, well-built chambermaid murmured a greeting as she finished tying back the curtains.

On the way out she stopped at the foot of the bed, gave him a deliberate, appreciative glance, then giggled and left. Gaunt discovered he'd kicked off the sheets and quilt during the night and, as usual, he'd slept naked. He looked down his body and grinned. At least the girl hadn't laughed.

It was 10 A.M. by his wrist-watch. He padded over to the window, saw a pale yellow sun already high in a cloudless blue sky, and felt totally rested. After going through to the bathroom, he stood under a cold shower long enough to let the icy needles of water bring him totally awake, rubbed himself dry with a towel, then went to dress.

A slip of paper was lying on top of his shirt. He picked it up and read the three-word message, "Take a walk."

He sighed, wondered just how many of the Smetana's staff had some connection with Janos Barta, and decided he'd better comply.

Ten minutes later he had shaved and dressed and took the elevator down to the ground floor. A city map in the hotel lobby showed him where the Old Town Square was located and he set off.

The air was cold outside, with hardly enough wind to flutter the limp flags or the red and gold banners. Gaunt walked briskly, the pavements busy, traffic in the streets a noisy mixture of rumbling tramcars and heavy trucks with private cars a minority. Most of the pedestrians were women with shopping baskets or shuffling old men but he stopped a few times, ostensibly to look in shop-windows, making sure he wasn't being followed.

The Old Town Square was only a few minutes away. Big and broad, its cobbled area was already crowded with groups of tourists who had come to see the Town Hall's famous astronomical clock strike the hour—the moment when medieval ingenuity would come to life, with the twelve apostles going past its little windows while a cock crowed and death tolled the passing of time.

Joining them, Gaunt stared dutifully at the intricacies of the clock's ornate structure. Cameras clicked around him, people gossiped and laughed, children ran about, and as the hands of the clock made their slow, deliberate circuit he wondered just how long it would be before Barta showed.

"Mister." An elbow nudged his side and a fat, shabbily dressed young man grinned at him. "You speak English?"

Gaunt nodded.

"Okay." The grin widened. The fat youngster brought a hand out from his overcoat pocket, clutching a fat wad of Czech banknotes. "English pounds, American dollars—you want a good rate, more spending money?"

"How good?" Two uniformed policemen stood in a doorway a short distance away. Both looked bored, one had his thumbs hooked into his pistol belt, the other was smoking a cigarette.

"The best, mister," declared the fat youngster. "Double your hotel rate—maybe a little more, eh?"

"What about the law?" Gaunt nodded slightly towards the policemen.

"No problem." The youngster winked significantly. "You know what I mean?" He edged closer, thumbing the wad of money in his grip, his expression unchanged, but his voice a sudden murmur. "Now tell me to get lost, Mr. Gaunt. Take the small street on your left. Janos is in a café about two hundred metres along."

Gaunt swallowed then forced a quick scowl.

"Stop pestering," he said loudly, and added softly, "Thanks."

The youngster shrugged and ambled towards the nearest group of tourists. Over in the doorway, one of the policemen laughed.

The small street had a dilapidated air. Most of its few shops were boarded up, the others had grubby windows and unpainted woodwork. The café, when Gaunt reached it, was modest in size and simply, cheaply furnished. It was warm with a steam and cigarette-smoke atmosphere and once inside Gaunt saw Janos Barta sitting alone at a table about half-way down its narrow length.

"Had breakfast?" asked Barta as Gaunt settled into the chair opposite.

"No."

"You had a late night." Barta nodded a wry understanding. "A busy one, too, I believe." He rubbed a thumb along his unshaven chin. "My apologies for the charade in the square. When a situation is delicate it pays to be careful."

"You've plenty of helpers," said Gaunt pointedly.

Barta nodded. "That was Andros. In my spare time, when I'm not taxi-driving, I still teach a few young people—unofficially. Little gatherings in back rooms, to discuss philosophy."

"Dissidents?" asked Gaunt.

"Young, inquiring minds," corrected Barta. He gave a slight, sad smile. "They repay me in different ways."

He beckoned a waitress. She brought each of them a bowl of greasy vegetable soup, a mug of coffee, and a plate piled with slabs of dark grey bread.

"About last night," began Barta, eating while he talked, "it was unfortunate. Did you—yes, I think the expression is 'keep your nose clean' ?"

"As far as I know." The soup was better than Gaunt had expected, and he realized he was hungry. "How much did you hear?"

"The barest bones—one of my young friends is in the militia." Barta broke one of the pieces of bread and dipped it into the greasy soup with fastidious care. "That an OBZ agent was stabbed, that the killers got away in a car, that you—ah—blundered into the situation. Why? Is there more?"

Gaunt nodded.

"I see." Barta's round face became serious, his tired eyes hardened behind the spectacles. "Well?"

"A link to Maggie Dimond." Quietly, Gaunt gave the chubby, grey-haired figure a brief outline of what had happened. He finished, then added soberly, "Brozman worries me."

"He worries most people," said Barta tartly. He paused, puzzled. "Why didn't you tell him you recognized this man Garr?" Then he understood. "Of course—I'm being stupid. That would bring its own problems. But I can tell you what I would do now."

"Take the next plane home?" suggested Gaunt sardonically.

"That would be too sensible a solution." Barta grinned a little. "No, I would ask myself if the woman and Garr are working together, or if the woman only thinks it is that way. That would leave the bearded stranger who visited her room as—"

"As the key to what it's really all about?" Gaunt finished it for him and swore under his breath. "Yes—that way it could make sense."

"Probability," corrected Barta. "There's a difference."

There was. But the Swiss merchant banker had to have a strong motivation for being in Prague. If his target the previous night had been the bearded man, then other things followed—particularly if even Garr didn't know the full story behind Maggie Dimond's visits to Czechoslovakia. The Czech security man could have been murdered because he blundered on Garr and his hired help at the wrong moment.

Gaunt pursed his lips at that thought. If his way out of the Smetana hadn't been blocked then it might not have been Brozman's man who died. He could be the one now lying on a mortuary slab.

"It all still comes back to Maggie Dimond," he said slowly. "I've got to wait until she makes a move."

"Which won't be this morning," murmured Barta, wrapping both hands round his coffee mug. He took a sip, his spectacle lenses misting in the process. "The lady is behaving exactly as a tourist should. At nine this morning she left the Smetana on an excursion bus—a sightseeing trip to the mountains. I saw her get aboard." He paused and gave a reassuring grunt. "It's a regular trip, with just one coffee stop, and there's a courier aboard to make sure no one strays."

Gaunt frowned. "When do they get back?"

"In time to have lunch at the Trade Fair exhibition," said Barta with total confidence. "Then they have a choice—either they stay at the exhibition, or a bus will take them to Prague Castle. They make their own way back." He gave Gaunt a wise smile. "If I wanted to meet someone, I would choose the castle. It is big and busy, and you expect a tourist to go there."

Gaunt nodded. If a meeting was on Maggie Dimond's mind, the castle sounded an ideal rendezvous.

"Where did you leave your cab?" he asked. "You've got a passenger."

His cover story for being in Prague had been to visit the Trade Fair. Like Maggie Dimond, he thought it a good time to do the expected thing.

Janos Barta drove a dark-green four-door Skoda, small and rusty, with an engine that laboured noisily and smoked an oily exhaust. But whatever he'd been like as a psychology lecturer, he knew how to handle a car. With Gaunt beside him in the front passenger seat, he headed west out of the city centre.

The day was still bright, and cold. After crossing a bridge over the Vltava, the little Skoda turned south on the broad road which ran parallel with the river bank and settled into the traffic pattern. Barges were moving on the river, big and deeply laden, their powerful diesel engines throbbing as they pushed against the current. Ducks bobbed on the water, women pushed prams along the riverbank paths.

"Ordinary," said Barta suddenly, as if reading Gaunt's mind. He smiled. "You see, we are ordinary. Most of us anyway—hell, even your average Russian is probably that way too, eh?" He drove on for a moment in silence then took one hand from the steering wheel and gestured ahead. "That's ordinary."

They were passing a wayside shrine, the stone old and worn, the statue of the Virgin in its shelter equally old, ending in a broken stump of neck, the head missing. But there were fresh flowers at the statue's feet.

"The usual treatment," said Barta mildly. "A swing of a sledge-hammer—not official policy, but a good Communist knows what to do." He shrugged. "Religion doesn't worry me, but as long as people bring flowers, who cares about sledge-hammers?"

They drove on for a few kilometres, left the river-side, and travelled through an area of parkland and housing blocks. Their destination was on the far side, a bold sprawl of large modern buildings. Notice boards in several languages proclaimed they'd reached the Strahov sports complex, home once every five years to the Spartakiada, the Czechoslovak festival of gymnastics.

"Sixteen thousand idiots jumping up and down to music," grumbled Barta. "*Za mir, za Socialismus*—all thinking with their muscles. That's why they built the exhibition centre out here—it can double for indoor events."

The building they stopped outside was like a giant concrete aircraft hangar, simple and severe in style, fronted by plain concrete pillars hung with banners. There was a car-park opposite, and a steady trickle of people were going in past the police guards on the main door.

"Could you be around after lunch?" asked Gaunt.

"Filled with *benzina* and ready to go." Barta nodded then

frowned as Gaunt reached for the door handle. "Except this still happens to be a taxi." He eyed the notes Gaunt pushed into his hand and chuckled. "I'll keep the change. You wouldn't win any prizes for tipping."

Getting out, Gaunt walked across a covered-in pavement, passed the police guards, and entered the exhibition hall through one of its sets of revolving doors.

Inside, it was like arriving in a vast Aladdin's Cave of industrial hardware. A warm, bright cave with long avenues of stands and exhibits, display boards and spotlights. A long-legged girl in a red-and-white uniform stopped him, greeted him in German, then tried English, smiled when he nodded, and presented him with an English-language exhibition catalogue. He thanked her, used the catalogue map to locate the electronics section, then headed in that direction.

There were fewer visitors around than he'd expected, and plenty of competition for their interest. Most stands seemed to be operating a free bar, the clink of glasses particularly fierce around a tractor stand, where salesmen had trapped a group of potential customers. Further along a display of heavy electrical plants offered a film show, and an ornamental fountain fronted a chemicals presentation.

Gaunt kept moving, threading his way through the long avenues. Overhead, a public address system alternated low, soft music with regular, frantic messages in a variety of languages, none apparently of interest to anyone.

The electronics section was on the north side of the hall, with an area to itself. The atmosphere there was, on the surface at least, more restrained. Each stand was guarded by barrier ropes and attendants and the equipment on display included several small working models and carefully spaced banks of flickering visual display units. Carol Marek was at one. She was wearing a lady-executive-style dark-blue skirt and jacket and talking to a beaming middle-aged technician.

An attendant unhooked a barrier rope to let him through. Carol saw him approaching, murmured an apology to the technician, and came straight over.

"I'm glad to see you," she said with unconcealed relief. "Jonny, couldn't you have let me know?"

"About what?" he asked mildly.

"About what happened to you last night," she said, almost angrily. Then she bit her lip, her indignation fading. "I'm sorry. But I only found out half an hour ago, when Colonel Brozman told me."

"He's here?" Gaunt didn't hide his surprise.

"Drifting around, being friendly to all mankind—particularly if they're women," she said. "He doesn't exactly want to give you a medal, but he says you could have been killed."

"Someone was," said Gaunt.

She nodded. "A local businessman—the police seem to think it was some black market quarrel."

"This 'local businessman' was working for Brozman," said Gaunt. "Remember the man at the baggage pick-up? The one Maggie Dimond tried to cripple?"

Her eyes widened. She stood silent for a moment, the electronic screens flickering in the background, units pulsing and quietly chattering all around them. She moistened her lips.

"Why?"

As briefly as he could, Gaunt told her. She bit her lip as he finished, then, silently, beckoned him to follow her. She led the way into a small reception room behind the computer displays, smiled briefly at the handful of sales executives and visitors already there, and went up to the drinks table at the far end. A word with the barman, and he poured two stiff measures of a clear liquor from a squat dark-green bottle.

"Yours." She passed one glass to Gaunt, nursed the other for a moment. "All right, I believe you."

"That's worth celebrating, I suppose." Gaunt sampled his drink then fought back a gasp as the liquor burned his throat and almost brought tears to his eyes.

"*Becherovka*," said Carol. "Most people say it's an acquired taste."

"Most people are right," said Gaunt hoarsely, the taste lingering as the fire died. "What is it—vodka with horns?"

"No, it's no relation. It's distilled from berries." Some of the others in the room were watching with amusement. Carol spoke to them in Czech and their grins widened. She turned to him again. "That's the commercial product. Go out into the farming areas, where they make their own, and it's stronger."

"God help them," said Gaunt. He paused respectfully as Carol took a long swallow from her glass. "Celebrating anything else?"

"Here?" She took a glance round and lowered her voice. "They've nothing on offer that Trellux need worry about. The quality's good but most of what they've got is bulky, and they're behind us in software."

"Which should please Eric Garfield."

"Yes." She looked at him oddly for a moment then shrugged. "There's a microswitch development that might interest him enough to order—the pricing seems reasonable."

Gaunt abandoned the rest of his *Becherovka* and they drifted out into the main stand area again.

"Where was Brozman last time you saw him?" he asked.

"Over there." She pointed vaguely towards the start of an industrial equipment gallery, then frowned. "Why? What are you going to do?"

"Make a polite noise and keep moving." He grinned at her. "How would you like a trip to Prague Castle after lunch?"

She wasn't deceived. "Maggie Dimond?"

"If she does what I expect. She's on a bus tour, stopping here over lunch."

Slowly, reluctantly, Carol shook her head. "I've work to do, appointments to keep. Anyway, if you're on your own—"

He nodded. It might be better. "Dinner tonight, then?"

"A certain lady permitting?" She nodded wryly. "If you're paying this time."

Gaunt left her and walked the length of the industrial equipment gallery without seeing any trace of Brozman. But as he turned off, on the start of a row of vehicle accessory stands, he faced the unwelcome sight of John Alford coming towards him.

"Having a good day, Gaunt?" Alford didn't wait for an answer. "I am. The poor sods on these stands have sales targets to meet or they're for the salt-mines. I've screwed down two deals already—left them sick at the terms, but that's their hard luck. Buy you a drink?"

"Sorry." Gaunt shook his head. "I've things to do."

Alford shrugged. "I've a wife to meet, that's all. She went off on a bus trip." He winked. "With my kind of luck, they'll bring her back."

Gaunt smiled weakly and escaped him. Even a stand devoted to metal castings looked more inviting. It took another few minutes of aimless strolling before he spotted Colonel Brozman, his height and close-cropped grey hair highlighting him as he stood talking to a group of Asians who had several business-suited Czech management in close attendance.

Brozman saw him a moment later, gave a casual nod, and came to meet him.

"What do you think of our little exhibition, Mr. Gaunt?" asked Brozman, smiling pleasantly. "We don't have all the promotional techniques of the West, but we try."

"I'm no particular expert—" began Gaunt.

"No?" The man's smile didn't change. "I thought you were something of an authority. In fact, my information was your Government sent you over to assess our modest ideas." He cocked his head a little to one side, like a benevolent, grey-topped bird of prey. "Or did the lady who told me have it wrong?"

Gaunt cursed himself mentally and forced a grin. "What's the local penalty for spying, Colonel?"

"None," said Brozman blandly. "Being caught is another matter." He chuckled and slapped Gaunt lightly on the back. "Speaking for our Foreign Office, I think we should feel flattered." His manner changed. "But it makes me regret last night's happening even more. We'll—ah—still need that statement to the police."

"Any time." Gaunt found his cigarettes and lit one, to give his hands something to do. "What about the man who was killed?"

Brozman's eyes hardened but his attitude remained amiable.

"The police believe it was a local matter." He shrugged. "Capitalist society has no monopoly on crime, Mr. Gaunt. Socialist democratic principles merely seek to create conditions where it is unnecessary."

"Marx?"

"No." Brozman dismissed the motion briskly. "The thoughts of Anatole Brozman. Some aspects of Marxist philosophy are becoming outdated, old-fashioned." As he spoke, the public address music faded and yet another message rasped from the loudspeakers. He sighed and glanced at his wrist-watch, a slim gold digital model. "That was for me. Good luck with your spying, Mr. Gaunt. We'll talk about it again."

Gaunt stayed where he was while the tall security officer strode off in search of a telephone. An elderly woman in overalls came along, a scarf tied over her hair, stooping over a brush, half-heartedly sweeping litter from the aisle, muttering to herself. A group of German businessmen strode past, deep in fierce discussion.

For the first time, Gaunt realized he was being watched. The man wore a brown suit. He was two stands away, half-hidden behind a coloured wire-and-globes model of some chemical compound. Carefully, unhurriedly, Gaunt took another draw on his cigarette then dropped the stub and ground it out under his heel.

He looked again, a casual glance.

The man was still behind the molecular mock-up's flimsy shelter. There was something vaguely familiar about his build and harsh, high-boned Slav features. Then the truth came with a startling clarity, from the previous night—he was one of the pair who'd struck down Brozman's agent.

Slowly, deliberately, Gaunt opened the exhibition catalogue. He flicked through a few pages then closed the catalogue and tucked it under his arm.

The man had gone. Probably to report back to Matthew Garr, report that Gaunt had been talking with a senior STB officer. The thought brought a twist of a grin to Gaunt's lips.

Even Swiss logic might have trouble sorting that out.

Though due back at twelve-thirty, Maggie Dimond's coach tour ran late. It was after one when the bus at last arrived at the front entrance to the Strahov hall, where several people had been waiting for it with varying degrees of patience. An irate courier was first out. He stood scowling as his passengers alighted.

Watching, wondering if Janos Barta's optimism had been misplaced, Jonathan Gaunt gave a sigh of relief as Maggie Dimond appeared from the vehicle.

"What the hell kept you, boy?" demanded an Australian voice as a red-haired teenager, one of the first off, reached them. "I've been standing here like an idiot, starving and thirsty—and damned near freezing."

"Women," said the teenager disparagingly. He thumbed at the bus. "One of them got herself lost at the coffee stop, what else? Half-way up a mountain, and she goes for a flamin' walk."

"Might have known," said his father with resignation. "Which one?"

The boy turned. "The fat, small one. She's getting off now."

It was John Alford's wife. She gave the fuming courier a friendly smile as she passed.

"What happened?" Gaunt asked the teenager.

"She strayed off." The boy grinned. "Got among some trees and couldn't find her way back. Silly old bag—the courier found her. Says she could have gone over a ledge and broken her neck." He turned to his father. "You said food, didn't you, Dad?"

The bus party had two long reserved tables in the exhibition hall's cafeteria. Maggie Dimond ate there, her tweed coat draped carelessly over the back of her chair. There were a few empty places. Alford's wife, for one, had been collected by her husband and taken in the direction of the nearest bar.

The cafeteria was big and busy. Gaunt found a seat at a corner table, sharing it with some Hungarians who were ordering a rough red wine by the carafe and who insisted on his sampling a glass. He ordered a sandwich and ate slowly, keeping an eye on Maggie Dimond. There was no sign of the man who'd watched him earlier, and Colonel Brozman didn't appear.

Eventually, Maggie Dimond left with two other women who'd been her table companions. Gaunt gave them a moment then paid his bill and followed, staying well back. Together, the three women made a leisurely way through the exhibition hall towards the main door, pausing occasionally to glance at one of the stand displays.

The same excursion bus was waiting outside. Loitering in the shadow of one of the tall concrete entrance pillars, Gaunt watched the three women join the trickle of people getting aboard. Some were people who'd been on the morning excursion, others were strangers.

The bus door began to close, then opened again as a last-minute passenger hurried out of the hall and scrambled aboard. It was the man with the brown suit and Slav features.

The bus began to pull away. Coming out from behind the pillar, walking past the police guards, Gaunt headed towards the line of taxis on the other side of the road. The first driver in the line grinned expectantly but Gaunt shook his head, walked on to where Janos Barta's old Skoda was waiting, and got in beside him.

"Follow it?" asked Barta. He was slouched back in the driving seat, an opened magazine lying on his lap.

"Yes." Gaunt sat tight-lipped while Barta dumped the magazine on the floor, started the old taxi, and set it moving.

"Is there a problem?" asked Barta after a few moments as they left the exhibition area. The Skoda was moving at an unhurried pace, the bus some distance ahead and almost out of sight.

"Too many cats chasing the same mouse," said Gaunt. "There's one on that bus."

"I see." Barta pursed his lips in a silent gloomy whistle. "But you still don't know why?"

Gaunt shook his head.

"Except it's bigger than you thought?" Barta's unshaven face creased in cynical amusement. "With women, it's always been that way. At the castle, you'll see what looks like an oversized metal birdcage in the main courtyard. One of our old kings had it built centuries ago. When any of the ladies of his court displeased him or were unfaithful, he locked them in it for a spell—a few days, a few weeks. At least that way he knew what they were doing."

"Try that on Maggie Dimond, and she'd probably have a skeleton key hidden in her bra," said Gaunt sourly.

Barta laughed and fed the Skoda a shade more accelerator.

By any standards Prague Castle was impressive. The cold spring sunlight adding an extra dimension to its splendour, a thousand years of Slav history built into its walls, the old stronghold of the Holy Roman Empire and the Habsburgs looked down on the city from across the river with the tall spire of St. Vitus Cathedral close in the background. Kings and princes might have been abolished, but the castle still mattered as much more than a tourist attraction. The soldiers on sentry duty at the main gates were a reminder that it was now the formal seat of the President of the Czech republic and the meeting-place of the Central Committee of the Czech Communist Party.

The Trade Fair bus drew in beside other coaches at a large, cobbled parking area near the gates. The parking area for cars and taxis was nearby and Janos Barta eased his Skoda into an inconspicuous space near the rear of the lines of vehicles.

"I'll be here," he said. "If you come back, fine. If you don't"—he shrugged—"well, maybe I can pick up another fare, eh?"

"Thanks," said Gaunt caustically.

Maggie Dimond's bus had emptied. As it drew away, leaving, its passengers began straggling across to join the other visitors going through the entrance gates. Maggie Dimond was out in front, striding briskly, her tweed coat flapping loosely. Further back, but not leaving too big a gap, the man in the brown suit ambled in pursuit. He was glancing around, his manner casual but as if wanting to make sure of something.

His hand already on the passenger door, Gaunt hesitated—then saw why, and swore under his breath.

Two men had stepped out of a dark-blue Polski-Fiat parked a few rows ahead of the Skoda. One was tall, young, and wore a grey duffel jacket. The other was smaller, broader, wearing a black fur hat, his coat collar turned up as if to protect him against the cold. But just for a moment, as he turned to speak to his companion, his scarred face was clearly visible.

Matthew Garr had surfaced. The Swiss merchant banker was coming out into the open.

Biting his lip, watching them start towards the gates, Gaunt remembered the last-moment way in which Maggie Dimond's shadow had just managed to board the Trade Fair bus. It was the kind of late arrival which could have been caused by a quick telephone call, a confirmation that Maggie Dimond had boarded, that the castle visit was scheduled—and perhaps that Gaunt, his other interest, wasn't travelling.

"We're in business." He saw Barta's puzzled expression and pointed ahead. "These two—you saw the car they came from?"

Barta nodded.

"Watch it. Whatever you see happening, don't get involved—but don't lose it."

He left the car before Barta could reply. Following Garr's example, he turned up the wide collar of his old sheepskin jacket and began walking, hands thrust deep in his pockets.

In through the castle gates, the main courtyard busy with what looked like an organized party of several dozen schoolchildren snaking their way through the other visitors, he found it easy enough to keep track of the bobbing black fur hat that was Matthew Garr. On ahead, he occasionally caught a glimpse of Maggie Dimond's distinctive tweed coat.

The schoolchildren had halted round the big metal woman-cage Barta had described. Maggie Dimond wasn't stopping, and seemed to know exactly where she was heading.

Two tall, cream-fronted blocks of castle apartments lay ahead, their red-tiled roofs almost touching, a narrow passage running between them. Few visitors seemed interested in what lay in that direction but Maggie Dimond strode purposefully towards the gap and vanished into its shadows.

Glancing back, the man in the brown suit signalled. His companion with the grey duffel jacket hurried forward and took over. As he disappeared in turn, Garr and the other man ventured in the same direction at a more sedate pace. The tail on their target had been switched, with a classic simplicity.

Drawing a deep breath, Gaunt headed after them with a sense of gathering tension. But before he could get to the gap a door on his left opened and a small swarm of camera-laden tourists emerged, shepherded by a woman guide. In a moment they surrounded him, heading in the same direction, the woman guide urging them on as if she was working to a tight schedule.

Going along with them, Gaunt saw another, equally large courtyard open out ahead. Garr and his companion had stopped short of the entrance, keeping close to the shelter of a wall, their attention fixed on what lay beyond.

Chattering, laughing, a mixture of nationalities, the tourist group swept past them with Gaunt deep in the middle, head turned away.

The courtyard was circular in shape, more castle apartments all around, passageways radiating out from it to run between them like the spokes of a giant wheel. An ornate stone fountain sat in the very middle, surrounded by a line of benches.

One man sat there, alone, waiting. He had a yellow anorak and a beard. He was the man who'd left Maggie Dimond's hotel room the previous night, and she was walking straight towards him.

The tourist group had slowed and some were taking photographs. Gaunt looked around quickly and saw what he'd feared. The other member of Matthew Garr's team was over to the far left, taking a deliberate, curving path close into the buildings on a route which would bring him behind the fountain. One hand was deep in a pocket of his grey duffel coat, his attention was totally fixed on the fountain area. Once he got far enough round, he could cut off any possibility of escape for the widow and her friend.

They were oblivious to that. The bearded man had risen from his bench and was greeting her with a smiling hug.

Dry-lipped, Gaunt glanced back. Garr and his other companion had quit the shelter of the passageway and were moving in, coming on slowly, using the tourist group as cover. They were only yards away from him, not much more than a long stone's throw from the fountain.

In the same instant, Garr saw him and registered immediate recognition. The scarred face twisted in surprise, his eyes widened, and the Swiss began shoving forward. Suddenly, as far as Gaunt was concerned, any choice had gone.

"Maggie!" He darted forward, shouting as he brushed past the startled guide. "Break for it. To your right—fast!"

She spun round, saw Gaunt, stared at him, then grabbed the bearded man by the arm and they began running.

Behind Gaunt, a woman screamed and a man swore in loud protest. Elbowing their way forward, Garr and his companion became tangled for a moment with angry tourists. Across the courtyard, the man in the grey duffel jacket stood bewildered.

Maggie Dimond and her bearded friend reached one of the courtyard exits. Gaunt sprinted after them, took a last glance back before he plunged into a narrow alley-way and saw the man with the duffel jacket running hard in the same direction. Whatever was happening to Garr and the second man, they still hadn't escaped from the confusion near the fountain.

He ran on. The alley-way had a slippery, moss-covered surface and curved and bent between high, blank stone walls. Rounding one bend, he caught a glimpse of a tweed coat as the two ahead hurried on.

But another smaller alley led off to the left. He paused, heard rapid footsteps catching up with him, footsteps that echoed off the stone walls, and sighed. A moment later, the man in the duffel jacket pounded into sight, still in hot pursuit.

Gaunt ran again, taking the left-hand way, hearing the man follow, knowing he could not be more than thirty yards behind. Rounding another bend, he almost collided with a startled couple coming in the opposite direction, and kept going, trying to increase the gap.

Then, suddenly, the buildings ended. He was in the open, on a small platform, surrounded on three sides by low battlement walls, a long, crumbling flight of sandstone steps on the fourth side leading down to a lower level of the castle.

Tired of running, breathing heavily, he dived into the shelter of one of the battlement recesses, pressing back against the cold stonework. The running footsteps came nearer, then his pursuer erupted out onto the little platform.

The man took one look at the empty steps, understood, and swung round, drawing a heavy switch-blade knife from his pocket.

He saw Gaunt, and the blade clicked open. He had a thin face, thinning fair hair, and a twisted grin of triumph. Wordlessly, he came straight in and swung the knife in a raking, underarm slash aimed at Gaunt's middle.

Gaunt dodged clear. As if a mental switch had been thrown, he felt totally calm, almost standing back from reality as his reflexes took over. In his paratroop training, one part of unarmed combat tuition had been the responsibility of a rat-faced little Cockney sergeant instructor whose boast was he'd killed more men with a knife than most of his pupils had had hot dinners. He had the knife, his pupils had their bare hands, and there was only one way to graduate. Paratroop sergeants seldom played games.

His attacker came boring in again. Gaunt got clear, made it seem awkward, pretended to stumble, and in the process got the small of his back firmly against the battlement.

The man in the duffel jacket scented his kill. Lips parting in a wider grin, he rushed in, the switch-blade starting another stabbing swing. As he moved, Gaunt slapped both arms back, hands bracing against the stonework, and brought his right foot pistoning out, heel first.

He took the man low in the body, hard enough for the blow to sound like a dulled drum-beat, and felt the jarring impact all the way up his leg. The man sunfished back, air exploding from his mouth in an incomplete squeal of agony. Staggering blindly, still going backward, somehow still grasping the knife, he stumbed on the edge of the old, worn steps.

Then, losing his balance, arms waving, a new terror in his expression, he overbalanced and fell.

For a long moment, Gaunt heard him crashing and bouncing down the long flight of steps. Then there was silence.

Grimly, he walked forward and looked. Far below, half-way down the long flight of steps, a motionless shape lay crumpled against the battlement wall.

There was still no one else in sight. Hurrying down, Gaunt reached the spot. The man was dead, his head twisted at an obscene angle, his neck broken. The knife lay nearby.

Stooping, working quickly, Gaunt checked the dead man's clothing. He collected a cheap plastic wallet from an inner pocket of the duffel coat and took an automatic pistol from a shoulder holster. Stuffing the pistol into his trouser waistband, putting the wallet in beside his own, he glanced over the battlements.

There was a long drop on the other side, then a steep slope thick with bushes, certainly thick enough for his purpose. With a grunt, he heaved the dead man up off the steps, got him balanced against the stonework, then heaved.

The body crashed through the bushes below and was gone from sight. He tossed the knife after it, then froze as he heard a woman's voice.

She came into sight a moment later, toiling up the steps towards him, a toddler in her arms, another child, a girl of about four, clinging to her skirt. Their mother was young, she looked exhausted, and the child struggling along beside her was beginning to fret.

Staying where he was, Gaunt smiled at the woman as she reached where he stood.

"Want some help?" he asked.

She looked at him blankly. He ruffled the little girl's hair, thumbed at the steps, then lifted the child.

"Okay?"

Relieved, she nodded.

They went up the steps together, then started along the narrow alley-way. Half-way along it, two militiamen hurried towards them from the other end. They looked flustered, and didn't spare the little "family" a glance as they went past.

The woman stopped and gave Gaunt a long, deliberate inspection. Then she shrugged, shifted the child in her arms into a more comfortable position, and set off again.

Everything seemed normal when they reached the first of the courtyards and there was no sign of Matthew Garr. Keeping pace with the woman, the little girl in his arms making contented noises, Gaunt stayed on edge until they were out in the main courtyard, near the entrance gates. Then he started to lower the child to the ground.

The woman stopped him, shook her head, and gestured towards the gates. There were more militiamen there, standing a little way back from the steady trickle of departing visitors.

Hoisting the child up again, Gaunt walked on with the woman. As they approached the gates she began talking to him, her voice angry. Whatever she was saying, the nearest militiamen began grinning.

Through the gates, out into the street, she kept on for a short distance then stopped and signalled him to put her child down.

Gaunt did, gently.

"Thanks," he said softly.

The woman winked at him, then blushed as he kissed her cheek. Grabbing her older child by the hand, she hurried off.

Matthew Garr's Polski-Fiat was still in the parking lot, empty. Lighting a cigarette, fingers suddenly shaking, Gaunt took one long draw, let the smoke out slowly, and headed back to Barta's taxi.

CHAPTER 5

"I knew an American once," said Janos Barta gravely. "He taught philosophy at Princeton. His favourite claim was that most of humanity came under one of three empirical headings—fools, damned fools, and poor damned fools." He shook his head. "Jonathan, I think you roll them up into one."

A quarter of an hour had passed since Gaunt had tumbled into the rear seat of the Skoda taxi. He sprawled low across its length, sipping from a can of fruit juice Barta had produced from a paper bag jammed between the front seats. His back had begun hurting, which was inevitable and, for the moment, incidental.

Matthew Garr's dark-blue Polski-Fiat still sat empty near the front of the castle parking lot, and Gaunt was prepared to wait.

He had told Barta what had happened. The automatic pistol, a nine-millimetre Luger with a full eight-shot magazine, was now stuffed under the Skoda's rear-seat cushions and within easy reach if needed. The dead man's plastic wallet, minutely examined by Barta, had yielded a surprisingly thick wad of Czech banknotes, a colour photograph of a girl who had signed the name "Trudi" on the back, and a crumpled, receipted bill from a Prague restaurant dated two days earlier.

Barta had pocketed the money. Then he'd stepped out of the Skoda just long enough to drop the wallet, photograph, and restaurant bill down the nearest street drain.

The dead man, like most in his trade, had been travelling light. But the restaurant bill at least told them that he had been in Prague before Garr had left Britain.

"Which also means this Garr is well organized," grumbled Barta. Hunched unhappily in his driving seat, he polished his spectacle lenses on a grubby corner of handkerchief. "You don't know how many people he has working for him." He scowled. "Another thing, we should get rid of that gun. Perhaps I haven't told you, but I am a peaceful man. If the police or worse find it—"

"Your fingerprints aren't on it and you carry a lot of passengers," soothed Gaunt. He finished the last of the fruit juice, abandoned the can, and frowned across at the castle. According to Barta, there were several side entrances. Maggie Dimond and her friend could have left by any one of them, and the same held good for Garr. "Why don't you have a radio in this thing?"

"I had, twice," said Barta gloomily. "Each time it was stolen. Why do you want to protect this Dimond woman so much?"

"I'm not protecting anyone," protested Gaunt. He wasn't sure if it was true. In the castle, he'd acted on instinct, still wasn't sure if he would have done exactly the same again. "I gave her a chance, that's all."

"So now the woman knows about you—and so does Garr," said Barta, unimpressed. "Do me one small favour, my Scottish friend. Next time you decide to go into battle like some old-fashioned knight, use someone else's taxi." He sighed. "You still want to wait for Garr?"

Gaunt nodded. "Then we see what he does."

Swearing, Barta put his spectacles on again.

They waited another twenty minutes. The sentries were changed over at the castle gates, a thin flurry of snow came from the greying sky, tour buses arrived and others departed. Barta amused himself by pointing out a trio of smartly dressed young black-market money-changers who arrived on pedal cycles and began sniffing for business among the tourists. They were ignored by the sentries and the occasional patrolling militiaman.

Then, suddenly, he stiffened. Two figures were walking along the street towards the parking area. Matthew Garr still wore his black fur hat, the man in the brown suit was close beside him and looked half-frozen.

Staying down out of sight, Gaunt listened to Barta's steady commentary. The two men took their time about approaching the Polski-Fiat, as if making certain all was well. When they did get aboard, Garr was behind the wheel. Seconds later the engine fired and it drew away, turning left as it reached the roadway.

Humming under his breath, Barta started the Skoda and slid it into gear. Once they were clear of the castle, the other car some distance ahead with light traffic in between, he glanced in his rear-view mirror and grinned.

"You'd be more comfortable sitting upright," he said. "In Prague, we expect taxis to have passengers. Or is that strange?"

Gaunt chuckled and obeyed.

Their luck was in. The dark-blue Polski-Fiat kept at a steady pace, moving with the traffic flow. After a few minutes they had crossed the river by another bridge and almost immediately were driving down a broad main thoroughfare lined with hotels and shops, office blocks and airline offices.

"Vaclav Square," said Barta, concentrating on his driving in the thickening traffic, cursing as another taxi cut in ahead of him. He jerked his head. "And the old fellow himself—you call him Good King Wenceslaus. He got murdered for the right reasons, so they made him a saint."

Gaunt barely had time or inclination to spare the massive equestrian statue a glance before they had passed it. The car ahead turned south, the Skoda followed, and they joined a broad main highway. The Polski-Fiat's speed increased a little and Barta matched it, keeping plenty of traffic between them, and relaxing a little.

"He's heading out of the city," he explained over his shoulder. Then he winked at Gaunt through the rear-view mirror. "I think I could bet where he's going—but we'll see."

There were two trucks, a tanker lorry, a bus, and several cars as a moving buffer between them and Garr's vehicle. It stayed that way for a few kilometres, the heart of the city giving way to factory buildings then, in turn, industry gradually giving way to houses. Garr's car changed lanes, slowed, and began signalling for a right turn. Leaving the highway, it took a side-road between some trees.

Smoothly, confidently, Barta followed. Once in the side-road, he reduced the Skoda's speed to little more than a crawl as they passed between the trees. Then he stopped his taxi just before they ended.

"There." He nodded ahead. "The *autokemp*—what I think you call a motel."

It was a mixture. What had once been a large mansion-house now had hotel signs. Log cabins nestled on one side and the other wing of the building was flanked by a grass field occupied by trailer cara-vans and a few tents. Several cars were parked in front of the hotel, and the dark-blue Polski-Fiat had stopped in front of one of the cabins.

The cabin door opened. A man came out, greeted Garr and his companion, and all three went into the cabin. The door closed.

Barta switched off the Skoda's engine. Gaunt sat silent for a moment, the ache in his back still throbbing. He heard an occasional crackle from the cooling exhaust and a dog was barking somewhere.

"Well?" asked Barta, turning round. "What now?"

"That depends on what they think happened to their friend," said Gaunt slowly.

"The man you killed?"

"The man who died," corrected Gaunt. "I told you."

"He fell. My apologies." Barta's voice held a wisp of amusement. "So?"

"They could move, they may stay." Gaunt gnawed his lip for a moment, thinking. Either way, the military answer for Matthew Garr's situation was 'regroup.' His previous plans had to have been left in tatters. "There's another man in the cabin—"

"One, maybe more," said Barta. He scratched the grey stubble on his chin. "A drink and a gossip at the *autokemp* bar, and it should be easy enough to find out. Leave that to me, Jonathan. Maybe you should be worrying more about what your Mrs. Dimond thinks of you now. Suppose I drive you in towards the city, drop you where you can get transport, then double back here? I'll keep in touch."

It made sense. Gaunt nodded reluctantly and Barta reached for the starter.

The little Skoda taxi took him what seemed at least half-way back towards the centre of Prague. Then Barta pulled in at the kerb outside a Metro station.

"Go carefully," warned Gaunt as he got out. "If there's any risk, vanish."

"What else?" commented Barta cheerfully.

The Skoda pulled away, making a defiant U-turn almost under the nose of a giant truck-and-trailer unit. Shaking his head, remembering too late he'd left the Luger still hidden in the rear-seat cushions, Gaunt went into the Metro station.

Prague's underground Metro system would one day be a spider's web of tunnels. But it was still modest in size, brand-new enough for workmen to be busy with final touches to the station's glinting green-tiled walls. One of the automatic coin-entry machines had broken down.

The station was busy, the day shift at a local factory on their way home. Gaunt strap-hung most of the way to the city centre, got out, took wry note of the nuclear attack deep-shelter signs along the platform, and was propositioned twice by young free-lance money-changers before an escalator took him to street level.

He was only a short walk away from the Hotel Smetana. When he arrived, the Hussar doorman gave him a smiling salute. There were no messages waiting for him at the desk when he collected his key, and the only face he recognized in the lobby area was one of the previous night's prostitutes, curled up in an armchair reading a book. Sharing an elevator up to the eighth floor with a Russian major in full uniform, he promised himself a drink as he reached his room and put the key in the lock.

The door opened on darkness. The curtains had already been closed. Fumbling for the light switch, he kicked the door shut behind him.

"Good evening, Mr. Gaunt," said an all too familiar voice an instant before the lights clicked on.

"Good evening," he replied automatically, staring.

Maggie Dimond sat in an armchair beside the TV set, totally at ease, legs crossed in front of her, a drink in one hand. Her face void of emotion, she gestured towards the little bar cabinet beside the bed.

"I helped myself. You don't mind?"

"No." Going over, he opened the cabinet. An emptied miniature of whisky met his eyes on the top shelf. It had been the only one. He opened one of a row of Czech brandies, poured it into a glass, then turned to face her. "How did you get in?"

"Bribed a maid." Maggie Dimond said it casually but every word was carefully controlled. "I want to know who the hell you are, Mr. Gaunt. After that—yes, I may thank you for this afternoon. I'm not sure yet."

"How about your friend?" asked Gaunt. "Couldn't he come along too?"

She shrugged, reached down with her free hand, and made a small, deliberate adjustment to the edge of her skirt.

"I felt it wasn't necessary." She sipped her drink and looked up at him. "I'd be happier if you sat down. I don't like men standing over me—particularly when they're scowling."

"All right." Gaunt sat on the edge of the bed. "But answer me something, Mrs. Dimond. You saw Matthew Garr back there?"

"At the castle?" She looked away from him for a moment. "Yes. We—it was a shock. But—"

"You ran." He cut her short. "You ran like a rabbit. Ran from a man you ate dinner with before you left Scotland. Why? Did you suddenly realize it must have been Garr who tried to snatch your other friend last night?"

"Perhaps." For a moment, her eyes showed that the mention of Scotland had got home. Then a wisp of humour entered her voice. "I've often been called a bitch. A rabbit is something new." Using both hands to nurse her drink, she took another sip and watched him over the edge. Suddenly she sounded weary. "Do we have to play games, Mr. Gaunt? Who are you, why are you here?"

"I work for an old-fashioned boss in Edinburgh." Gaunt took a gulp of his brandy and the fiery liquor spread a quick, welcome warmth through his body. His back began to feel a little less like it had been through a mangle. "He's called the Queen's and Lord Treasurer's Remembrancer. One of the jobs we do now and again is check on people like you, Mrs. Dimond."

"I don't understand," she said. But her expression had changed.

"No?" Gaunt sighed. "Inland Revenue don't like discovering that someone on their staff is up to her neck in tax evasion. You and I—maybe we see it differently. But they'd be happier if you'd committed murder."

"You mean it?" She stared at him. "You followed me out to Prague just because someone thinks I'm tax-dodging?"

"Yes."

"My God." She gave a noise like a strangled laugh. "That—and what else?"

"Whatever else there is," he said softly. "Someone shopped you, Maggie—the anonymous way."

"Somebody?"

He shrugged. "You're due for promotion soon, aren't you?"

"Yes." Her mouth showed odd amusement for a moment. "I think I understand. What was wrong with calling me in for an interview, asking me?"

"Would Inland Revenue do it that way with John MacPublic?"

"No," she admitted. "We like to know the answers before we ask the questions." She moved in the chair, her copper hair glinting under the room light. "I asked what else."

"A pattern." Gaunt saw no sense in holding back. "You start travelling back and forward to Prague. At the same time, you start spending money, a lot of money. It keeps coming in—and you keep coming out here." He paused, remembering what he'd said to Falconer back in Edinburgh. "Maggie, you didn't earn that kind of money moonlighting over tax accounts. You found a money tree in Prague."

"Did I?" She took a deep breath, an angry glint in her eyes. "Doing what?"

Slowly, deliberately, Gaunt took out his cigarettes and lit one. As an afterthought, he offered the pack. Maggie Dimond shook her head.

"Inland Revenue doesn't exactly rate as a security risk area," he said. "You're clear on that count—or that's what I was told." He drew on the cigarette briefly. "I still don't know what you're doing. To be honest, I don't particularly care. But you're in trouble, Maggie. Up to your neck in trouble."

"You're wrong about the money," she said. Getting up, she paced the room for a moment then came back and glared down at him. "Yes, the money exists, but has it earned any taxable income?"

He blinked, caught off guard.

"First, I'll tell you where it came from." She paused, and when she spoke again her voice was quieter, with a new, underlying emotion. "Your people would run a routine check—possible inheritances, the usual?"

"Yes." He nodded. "Thorough."

"Not thorough enough." She almost smiled, not at Gaunt, but as if at a memory. "Well, that's understandable. It was meant to be that way. You see, there was a man—an honourable, well-known man. He was married, he was wealthy, and his family mattered to him, mattered very much. I accepted that." She paused. "So did his wife—people can. Or do you find that hard to believe?"

"No." He meant it.

"Thank you." She gave an expressive shrug. "It stayed that way, Mr. Gaunt. I like my work, I'm not even sure I wanted to marry again. Then about three years ago he died suddenly, unexpectedly. In his will, he left me one quarter of his total estate—in net terms, about eighty thousand pounds."

Gaunt fought back a whistle. "The family—"

"Didn't object." Maggie Dimond gave a slight, unexpected chuckle. "All they wanted was to avoid scandal. That was easy enough. You see, he had been shrewd. Shrewd enough to pick an excellent tax haven."

"Where?"

"Ireland. That's where the will was confirmed." She smiled at him. "It takes time to wind up an estate. I received the first instalment of that money about two years ago. It's been coming in ever since."

"You could prove this?"

"If I had to, yes." She nodded. "Mr. Gaunt, I didn't want to make any particularly dramatic change to my life-style—but at the same time I wanted to invest that money, and I knew the best way to do that and keep clear of tax."

"Your job," said Gaunt dryly.

"Exactly." She nodded again. "First, the money came to me free of any tax liability. I didn't have to declare it. Then, if you lodge money in a current account with most British banks, it doesn't earn interest. Next, if you buy a house and it appreciates in value, British law says there's no tax on the profit provided it's the house you live in. The same no tax on profits rule applies to jewellery, gold coins, and plenty of other items. That's what I've done. I haven't broken a single law."

"I'll believe you." Gaunt ran a hand across his chin, his thoughts confused. But she had told him the truth—he was sure of that much. "And what about here, in Prague?"

"My affair, Mr. Gaunt." She shook her head firmly. "It doesn't concern you—not in any way. My word on that."

"You're wrong, Maggie." Gaunt stubbed his half-smoked cigarette, his voice harsher than he meant. "One of Garr's men was killed this afternoon."

"Killed?" Her eyes widened, more in surprise than horror. "Did you—"

"I'd say no. But it happened. Then another man was murdered last night." He couldn't hide his sarcasm. "I presume you do know about him?"

She bit her lip and nodded.

"How about who he was?"

"Someone local. I heard—"

"He was one of Colonel Brozman's men. Remember the character you decided was annoying you at the airport?" He saw she did. "Yes, that one. Your Swiss friend was there, and I walked into it. Then—you know about Brozman?"

"That he works for Czech security?" she met his eyes calmly. "Yes. He told me himself. At least, he dropped a hint."

"A hint, or a warning?"

"A hint—I hope." She surprised him with a smile, the kind which made her face younger and matched a bright determination in her eyes. "I don't think there's much danger."

"Then try thinking again." Gaunt scowled at her. "Brozman had a man on your plane coming out."

"Chance," she suggested.

"And the way your house was burgled before you left? The break-in you didn't report?"

"I—" She stared at him, open-mouthed. "You knew about that?"

Gaunt nodded. He saw no sense in adding he'd gone there intent on the same kind of mission.

"Garr," she said earnestly. "He was taking me out, he knew the house would be empty. The way Stepan and I see things now—"

He stopped her. "Stepan? He's the man you've been meeting?"

"Yes."

"And what's his speciality—apart from running?"

"Damn you, that's unfair." She reacted indignantly, as he'd intended. "Stepan is no coward. If you knew who he was, what he's trying to do—" Then she realized the trap and stopped there. "Let's leave it that we think it was Matthew Garr. It's our own fault. We needed someone with his kind of contacts, we offered him a business deal."

"But now he wants to take over?"

She nodded.

"Could he?"

"No." She was positive. "Garr knows hardly anything. He's only guessing."

"Suppose he got your friend Stepan?" persisted Gaunt. "How

good would Stepan be at standing up to little refinements like losing his fingernails one at a time?"

"That's not going to happen." Maggie Dimond made it a statement of fact. She glanced at her wrist-watch. "I have to go. But—well, your job here is finished now, isn't it?"

"I'll think about that," Gaunt told her.

"You should." She made it close to a plea. Then, glancing at her wrist-watch again, she said wryly, "At least I shouldn't have to worry this evening. I'll be in fairly safe company."

"Meaning?"

"I'm having dinner with Colonel Brozman." Maggie Dimond almost grinned at his expression. "Why not? I reckon I can cope with him."

"You probably can," agreed Gaunt.

He got to his feet and saw her to the door, opening it for her.

"Enjoy your evening," he told her.

"I intend to." Maggie Dimond looked at him for a moment then, unexpectedly, put a hand on his arm. "Thank you, Jonathan, for what you did this afternoon. I won't forget it."

She left, an erect, confident figure, heading for her room. Closing his door, Gaunt let out a long sigh.

His back still hurt. He caught a glimpse of his face in a mirror and scowled at the reflection. Back in Edinburgh, Henry Falconer would still want proof to back Maggie Dimond's story. But he believed it—as much as she'd told him. The Queen's and Lord Treasurer's Remembrancer's Department had got itself involved in a mess of someone else's trouble, the kind of trouble that could only keep growing.

Getting the bottle of pain-killer pills from the bathroom cabinet, he swallowed one. Another miniature of brandy from the bedside bar helped wash it down, then he sprawled back on the bed, trying to decide what to do.

Stay or get out—the choice was his. Sooner or later a dead man was going to be found among the bushes at Prague Castle. How long would it be after that before the Czech security police became involved? Then there was another, equally deadly factor to consider —Matthew Garr and his remaining men. Whatever doubts might have restrained the scar-faced Swiss had been wiped out that afternoon. He had killed before. Gaunt had no illusions about what was likely to happen if he strayed across Garr's path again.

Yet it wasn't so totally simple or cut-and-dried. He'd come to Prague to find out why Maggie Dimond kept going there. He'd only gone a very little way along that road, and he had a basic, stubborn dislike of giving up so inconclusively.

Henry Falconer might have pulled him out, brought him back. But Falconer would be viewing things from a desk in Edinburgh.

For a moment, he grinned at the ceiling. At least the longer he stayed away from home, the longer it was before he had to go back to the financial mess he'd left behind. The Czech side of the Iron Curtain didn't provide any service of Western stock exchange news. For all he knew, minor miracles might have been happening.

Except it was unlikely.

He stopped trying to think about anything, closed his eyes, and relaxed.

When the telephone rang, it seemed only a moment had passed. Yawning, he stretched across the bed and lifted the receiver.

It was Carol Marek. She said cheerfully, "Sorry it's so late. I got into a business hassle at the Trade Fair—I'm not long back."

"Late?" He glanced at his watch and blinked. He'd dozed off and had been asleep for almost two hours. "That's all right."

"You're still buying me dinner?"

"Unless you've had a better offer." He grinned at the receiver. "When?"

"Give me half an hour to feel human again," suggested Carol. She hesitated. "How about you, Jonny? This afternoon, I mean. Did things work out?"

"Yes, but not the way I expected," he admitted. "Why?"

"I've just had an over-the-balcony chat with the lady next door," explained Carol. "It seems she has a date for tonight. I thought you'd like to know."

"She told me," said Gaunt. "A certain colonel."

"Oh." Carol sounded disappointed. "Well, aren't you interested?"

"That's not quite the word," Gaunt told her.

"No, I didn't think it would be," she said mildly. "Half an hour?"

"I'll be along," he promised, and hung up.

Gaunt had a shower and changed his clothes. There was a Parachute Regiment tie in his bag, something he'd thrown in as a perverse, last-minute decision before he'd left. He considered it for a moment then, on a sudden whim, decided to wear it.

He was tying the knot when the telephone rang again. This time he answered it briskly.

"You asked me to call you, Mr. Gaunt," said a voice he recognized straight away as Janos Barta. "It's about that *autokemp* tourist information you wanted."

"I remember." Gaunt chose his words carefully, to match Barta's approach. "Are there any problems?"

"No, but I can give you more details." Barta broke off for a moment and Gaunt could hear a background murmur of voices over the line. "Could I see you later?"

"Where are you now?" asked Gaunt.

"In a bar—not too far away," said Barta. "There's no urgency."

"Fine." Gaunt thought for a moment. "I'm going out fairly soon, with a friend. She might like to meet you sometime."

"She?" Barta made it clear he didn't like the idea. Then he sighed. "I'll be in touch, Mr. Gaunt. We'll make an arrangement."

The line went dead. Hanging up, Gaunt slowly finished checking his tie, then frowned at the mirror. Maggie Dimond apart, self-protection made a very good reason why he still wanted Barta keeping tabs on Matthew Garr.

But there were doubts in his mind again. He'd already involved Carol Marek in a way that shouldn't have happened. Maybe the sensible thing would be to cut short his stay and take the first flight out to Britain the next morning, before something else happened.

Swearing under his breath, he stubbornly stopped it there. Like it or not, he wasn't finished. He might still end up going back to Falconer without a complete report, but he had to keep trying.

He went along to Carol's room at seven-thirty. When he tapped on her door she opened it, greeted him with a smile, and invited him in.

"I need another minute—and some help," she told him, closing the door once he'd entered. She turned away from him. "This damned zip's stuck. Have a try, will you?"

He grinned and obeyed. The last few inches of zip-fastener at the back of her pale-blue dress yielded to a firm tug and he finished the job, closing the tiny hook-and-eye fastening at the top. He lingered over it for a moment, his fingertips against the soft warmth of her skin, her dark hair brushing his hands.

"Thanks." Carol turned to face him, a twinkle in her brown eyes. "I get a feeling you've done that before."

"It's one of my skills." Gaunt watched as she crossed to the dressing table and gave her hair a last few flicks with a comb. "Was the afternoon a success?"

"At the Trade Fair?" She wrinkled her nose. "I'm earning my keep. Even Eric Garfield's going to have to admit it." She put down the comb. "How about you?"

"I had a talk." He thumbed at the wall which separated them from Maggie Dimond's room. "She knows why I'm here."

"Because you told her?"

He nodded. "After something happened."

"Something?" She considered him carefully, the laughter gone from her eyes, then nodded. "When you came in just now, I wondered. Maybe you were being too normal."

"That could be the reason I keep losing at poker." He smiled at her gravely. "It can wait till later. I thought we could eat out."

"I'd like that." She frowned a little. "It may not be so clever now, but I had an idea for afterwards—a theatre show. I asked the hotel desk to get two tickets."

"Any special reason?" He sensed there had to be.

Carol nodded. "Maggie Dimond and her colonel will be there." She eyed him uncertainly. "Well?"

"Why not?" He gave a slow, appreciative nod. "I might even enjoy it."

"Good." She had an afterthought. "I told the desk you'd pay."

They took the elevator down to the lobby, collected the theatre tickets at the reception desk, and left the hotel. There was a new flurry of snow outside the Smetana and the Hussar doorman was busy feeding a number of business-suited Dutchmen into the only two taxis which were waiting.

A third taxi came crawling in. Then another accelerated from out of nowhere, cut across its front, and stopped beside Gaunt and Carol with a squeal of brakes. Janos Barta looked out at them from the driving seat, ignoring an indignant horn-blast from the other driver.

"This one," said Gaunt resignedly.

He followed Carol into the rear seat, closed the passenger door, and Barta set the old Skoda moving again. Their eyes met in the driving mirror and Barta gave him a quizzical grin.

"Carol, say hello," suggested Gaunt. "This is Janos Barta. He has a gift for staying on the edge of trouble but never getting too close."

Barta chuckled, half-turned in his seat, and gave Carol a quick, appreciative glance through his spectacles. He asked a question in Czech and Carol laughed, then replied. Giving a satisfied grunt, Barta settled more comfortably behind the wheel.

"Someone translate that," said Gaunt suspiciously.

"I thought she was too pretty to be any kind of a British woman," said Barta complacently, his eyes on the road. "I was half-right, eh? Now—where do you want to go?"

"Somewhere we can eat."

"I know the place." Barta let the Skoda coast to a halt at traffic lights, next to a long, black limousine which had the passenger compartment curtains closed. "It's expensive." He thumbed at the limousine. "But their kind aren't welcome and the food is good."

"And you get a rake-off?"

"Naturally." The lights changed and Barta set the little taxi moving again. "This is Prague—and I have to live." He paused, then asked quietly, "Can we talk?"

Gaunt nodded. "Carol knows most of it."

"Including my part?" Barta frowned, then glanced at Carol through the mirror. "She appreciates I prefer not to advertise?"

Carol nodded.

"Good—and nothing personal intended. Trust is a fairly scarce commodity in this city." Barta took the Skoda through a right turn at a road junction then switched his attention back to Gaunt. "Garr hasn't left his chalet at the *autokemp*. One of my young people is keeping an eye on things there. The two men with Garr are named Leiber and Zelagny—both with Swiss passports and tourist visas, but Zelagny speaks Czech like a native."

"When did they arrive?"

"Last weekend. Garr joined them yesterday—a flight from Zürich, same travel documents."

Gaunt whistled softly. Matthew Garr had made some fast airport-hopping to achieve that kind of progress.

"And the one at the castle?"

Barta frowned at him in the driving mirror, an unspoken question in his eyes.

"No," said Gaunt, "I haven't told her—not yet."

"Haven't told me what?" demanded Carol, who'd been listening in silence. She moistened her lips. "Jonny, this afternoon—"

"One of Garr's men had an accident," said Gaunt.

"Fatal?" She wasn't deceived.

"Very," agreed Barta. "Otherwise, young lady, you might be eating dinner alone tonight."

"I see." Her voice didn't quite manage to stay steady. "What about the police?"

"So far they don't seem to have found him," said Barta with some satisfaction. "When he registered at the *autokemp* his name was Radiki—Swiss passport and papers like the others." He stopped talking for a moment, easing the Skoda through a traffic bottle-neck caused by a truck which had broken down. Past that, he turned into a street which ran along the river bank. "You want me to keep watching them, Jonathan?"

"Yes." Gaunt pursed his lips. "But go carefully."

"Rely on that, my friend," said Barta cheerfully. "Meet me for breakfast tomorrow. You get out here."

The restaurant was an old converted river barge moored to a wooden jetty, the cold water of the Vltava lapping against its hull. Small coloured lights decorated the main gangway but no other attempt was made to announce its existence.

They went aboard, into a restaurant area which was modest in size and plainly furnished. It was already busy. A waiter in a white sweater and blue jeans led them to a vacant table for two and placed a handwritten menu on the spotlessly clean red and white checked table-cloth.

"A drink first," suggested Gaunt.

They ordered. The drinks arrived and they sipped them in silence for a few moments. Then, at last, Carol broke her self-imposed silence.

"Will you tell me now?" she asked.

"About this afternoon?" Using the tip of one of the table-knives,

Gaunt drew a random pattern on the cloth. He looked at her doubt-fully. "Why?"

"I want to know," she said simply.

"That's honest." He came out of his musing, saw the waiter was still hovering, and waved him away for the moment. "I'll give you the basics."

He kept it that way, telling what had happened at the castle and afterwards in a few clipped, low-voiced sentences.

"That's it." Gaunt felt a gloomy satisfaction as he finished. "Don't ask me what's likely to happen next. I don't know."

"But something will." She bit her lip. "Can't you leave it, just—well, get out?"

He shook his head. The temptation was still there, no matter how hard he tried to bury it. On top of everything else, a new, uneasy feeling had entered his mind. Whatever Maggie Dimond's purpose was in Czechoslovakia, whatever way she protested her innocence, the British connection might have its own importance, could be a potential political embarrassment.

No, he wasn't finished in Prague.

"Then you'd better decide something else," said Carol resignedly. She pushed the menu in front of him and shaped a wry smile. "What are we going to eat?"

Barta had been right. The floating restaurant's food was as excel-lent as it was expensive, the service casual but efficient. They chose pork steaks in butter as a main course, served garnished with tiny diced vegetables and ornately shaped fragments of lemon. Dessert was a chocolate cake, laced with brandy and topped with cream.

They finished with coffee, Gaunt paid the bill, and he sat back for a moment, watching Carol. She was smoking one of her little cheroots. They'd kept to small talk during the meal, but once or twice he'd caught her off guard and had known her thoughts were far removed from idle conversation.

"Suppose we forget the theatre show," he said. "We can go back to the hotel—a straight goodbye, no hard feelings."

Carol blinked. She took a moment to stub the cheroot in an ash-tray.

"The tickets are paid for," she said indignantly, then grinned at him. "Why waste them?"

"Right." He returned her grin and shoved back his chair. "You'll need to translate."

"No." Carol shook her head, amused. "It's a *Laterna Magika* mime show—two hours, not a word spoken." She saw his dismay. "Think of it as an experience. You might even enjoy it."

They left the floating restaurant, hailed a taxi, and it was a five-minute journey from there through the centre of the city. Their driver used a succession of shabby back streets to avoid the traffic, but they still passed several two-man militia patrols and saw the inevitable prowling police cars.

Night-time was kind to Prague. It left her buildings and spires as clean, splendid silhouettes against the sky, hid or disguised her tired, down-at-heel shabbiness.

The mime show theatre was in the Old Quarter of the city. Gaunt paid off the taxi, helped Carol out, and took a glance at the few dog-eared posters on the plain stone frontage. Then he took her arm as they joined the flow of people going in.

The performance was due to start. A handful of middle-aged women in street clothes collected tickets, offered programmes, and gestured patrons in the general direction of their seats. Spartan in its comforts, with bare wooden flooring and plain, hard seats, the auditorium area was already well filled.

He let Carol lead the way. Their seats were in the middle of a row occupied almost exclusively by teenagers and a considerable percentage of the audience seemed to be either students or tourists. But Gaunt's interest rose a little as he noticed the impressive battery of amplifiers and effects units in front of the stage, which was backed by a full-width cinema screen. Whatever else the mime show might have to offer, it had plenty of technology.

"Smile, will you?" Carol dug him in the ribs. "They're to your left, near the front. Brozman's seen us."

Colonel Anatole Brozman was looking round from a seat close to the centre aisle in the third front row. Brozman waved, spoke to Maggie Dimond, who was on his left, and she turned just long enough to give a cool smile then went back to glancing at her programme.

"She's the warm and friendly type tonight," muttered Carol. "If she's worried about Brozman, she can have him." She gave a quick frown. "See anyone else who might matter?"

Gaunt shook his head. Around them the audience gradually settled as the house lights dimmed.

For the first few minutes after that, Jonathan Gaunt felt lost. Whatever he'd expected, he'd been totally unprepared for the assault on his senses that erupted from the *Laterna Magika* stage. Prerecorded sound and programmed, multihued lighting blended with split-screen cine film, music and live performers. Stage settings merged into filmed backdrops. Actors were on screen one minute, suddenly on stage the next, gone a moment later, never a word spoken.

The audience were hushed. There was no time, no chance for applause. The story hardly mattered—two circus clowns, hatched from eggs, following a beautiful girl on a pilgrimage of fantasy and pursued by a devil figure. It swept on, at a pace that always seemed to be quickening.

Then, as suddenly as it had begun, the performance reached the interval break. The house lights came back. There was scattered applause but like Gaunt most of the audience were still in a partial daze.

"You didn't tell me it would be like that," he accused Carol.

"No." She was pleased. "I saw it once before, with my father. I—it's better as a discovery." She broke off, her eyes narrowing with interest. "Your lady is making a move."

Maggie Dimond had left her seat and was going across the front aisle, towards one of the exit doors. Brozman was lounging back in his seat, showing every sign of staying that way.

"Powder room." Carol got to her feet and shook her head at Gaunt's half-formed protest. "If that's where she's heading, what can you do about it?"

She set off. Gaunt watched her vanish in the same direction, sighed, and picked up the programme booklet.

He was thumbing through its pages when a hand tapped his shoulder. He glanced round, and one of the women attendants stood behind him. She smiled, pointed across the theatre to her left, then handed him a folded slip of paper and went away again.

Puzzled, he unfolded the note. The message was three words long and unsigned: "Could we talk?"

He glanced round quickly, in the direction the woman had indicated. Over on the far side, standing next to a pillar, Maggie

Dimond's bearded partner met his gaze and gave a slight nod. Turning deliberately, he began to stroll slowly towards the back of the theatre.

Squeezing past the chattering students around him, Gaunt reached the nearest aisle and set off in the same direction. The bearded man didn't hurry, looked round once or twice, then went out through an archway into a corridor area.

When Gaunt got there, several theatre-goers were standing around, smoking and talking. But the bearded man seemed to have vanished. Swearing under his breath, he pushed his way through the other people and saw him again, standing further along, on his own, leaning against a fire door.

"Good evening, Mr. Gaunt." His voice was soft, pleasant, and held a hint of an accent which was almost American. "I thought you'd be interested."

"I like to know who I'm talking to," said Gaunt. "Maggie Dimond called you Stepan."

The bearded man shrugged. His hands were deep in the pockets of a black gabardine raincoat, which hung open and showed the grey sports suit he was wearing. The suit had a jacket cut hunting style, with high lapels, and beneath that he wore a black roll-neck sweater.

"My apologies," he said dryly. "I am Stepan Valachova. Introductions complete?"

"For now," said Gaunt.

"Good." Valachova nodded. "We couldn't issue a formal invitation, Mr. Gaunt. That's why Mrs. Dimond made sure a certain young lady knew where she'd be tonight." He chuckled at Gaunt's expression. "It happened like we expected."

"And?" Gaunt waited.

"You've come to my rescue twice." Valachova eyed him for a moment. "Now, the way things are, I want to suggest a—yes, an alliance." He eased his position against the scarred wood of the fire door. "And in case of wild thoughts, I have a gun in my right pocket."

"Everyone needs protection," said Gaunt. "You want to make a deal. What kind?"

"One that could earn you some money. I understand you killed a man today, Mr. Gaunt. You have—well, your own problems now.

Even if you decided that way, it would be difficult for you to say anything about me to Colonel Brozman. At the same time, Matthew Garr almost certainly believes you are working with Mrs. Dimond. So"—he gave another slight chuckle—"why not make the best of it?"

"Which is?"

"Five thousand British pounds—or its equivalent, in gold. Half when you cut short your visit and fly home. The rest when your employers get your report that Mrs. Dimond is an innocent victim of their suspicions." Valachova sighed a little. "Which is more or less true anyway, but we want rid of you, Mr. Gaunt."

"Suppose I'm not interested?"

"Then that would be a pity." In the theatre, the bell signalling the end of the interval began ringing. "I am not a particularly violent man, Mr. Gaunt—let me show you proof." His right hand came out of the raincoat pocket. His fingers were clutched round an old briar pipe. "But if anyone—Matthew Garr, or anyone else— threatens what I'm doing then I'm prepared to kill."

"How about Colonel Brozman?" asked Gaunt. "He's got a lot of back-up. Or are you thinking of starting a war?"

"You're from the West," said Valachova. "Live here, and you don't joke that way. Think about it, Mr. Gaunt."

Stepping back, he gave the fire door a sudden push. It swung open, he stepped out, and vanished in the shadows.

CHAPTER 6

A woman attendant found him standing beside the open fire door, gave a disapproving glare, and slammed it shut. The theatre bell had stopped ringing and he headed back towards his seat.

Carol had already returned. He settled beside her as the house lights dimmed and the second half of the *Laterna Magika* show got under way.

"Where did you disappear to?" she asked in a whisper.

"To talk to a man, by invitation," he told her. "Maggie's friend Stepan."

"Here?" Carol's eyes widened.

Gaunt nodded. "We were set up."

"Why?" A sound effects storm had got under way from the amplifiers beside the stage while spotlights stabbed and the mime artists reeled around. She mouthed as much as spoke. "What did he want?"

"To do a deal." Gaunt could just make out Maggie Dimond in her seat. "What about her?"

"Powder room—asked me if I was enjoying the show." Carol leaned close, speaking almost into his ear to defeat the noise. "Plenty of polite chat." She paused. "What kind of deal?"

"Go home, behave, and I'll get a nice present," said Gaunt.

"How nice?" She nudged him. "How much?"

"Tell you later." They were drawing annoyed glances from some of the people around. Gaunt smiled apologetically at the nearest scowling face. "Shut up, or we'll get thrown out."

Carol subsided.

The show went on in its fantasy mix of stage and film, sound and light. The two clowns, still its central characters, continued their pilgrimage in pursuit of the beautiful girl. They grew old, she didn't.

It ended that way, to thunderous applause. A girl student near Gaunt sat crying softly. At last, slowly, the theatre began to clear.

Somehow, it wasn't too much of a surprise to Gaunt that Colonel Brozman and Maggie Dimond were waiting for them at the exit.

"Did you enjoy the show?" asked Brozman pleasantly. He gave a wide smile as they nodded. "Good—then can I invite you both to join us for a drink?"

"Well—" Gaunt hesitated, then for an instant he saw a silent plea in Maggie Dimond's expression. "I'd like that. Carol?"

"If we're not intruding." Carol gave Maggie Dimond a cool, quizzical glance. "You're sure?"

"Of course," Maggie Dimond answered warmly. But once again her eyes were on Gaunt, the same plea there as before.

"Then lead the way, Colonel," said Gaunt. He looked directly at Maggie Dimond. "It's the best offer I've had today."

They left the theatre. Brozman guided them a little way down the street and indicated his car with an unmistakable touch of pride. It was a low-slung Porsche coupe, grey in colour, the model a few years old but well maintained, and the first Gaunt had seen with Czech licence plates.

"Your own?" asked Gaunt, remembering the big official Tatra he'd seen Brozman use earlier.

"Yes. I brought it back with me from my last posting in the West." Brozman opened the doors and stood back. "I call this car my one small extravagance in life. Do cars interest you, Mr. Gaunt?"

"When I can afford them." Gaunt winced a little at the reminder. "But not right now."

They squeezed aboard, Gaunt and Carol in the cramped rear seat, Maggie Dimond up front beside Brozman. The Porsche's twelve-cylinder engine fired and throbbed gently.

"Somewhere near, I think," said Brozman. He gave Maggie Dimond a sideways glance. "Near and—yes, relaxing in mood. Agreed?"

He blipped the accelerator then set the coupe moving.

The night-club was small, dimly lit, and on the first floor of a building just off Vaclav Square. It had leather-upholstered booth seating, a piano playing quietly in one corner, and an exclusive air which matched the well-dressed men and jewelled women who were its customers.

Two men wearing dinner jackets were on duty at the door. They murmured a greeting when they saw Brozman, then one led the way to a vacant booth.

"One of your regular haunts?" asked Carol as they settled.

"I use it quite a lot." Brozman gave a wisp of a smile. "Sometimes for business, sometimes for pleasure, Miss Marek. It can be useful for both."

"And tonight?" asked Gaunt.

"Pleasure, naturally." Brozman's voice held a mild indignation.

A hostess in a black-velvet, split-sided skirt and a white blouse that would have been demure if it hadn't been see-through took their order for drinks. She went away, showing she knew how to use her hips when she walked.

"Interesting." Brozman gave Gaunt a deliberate wink. "Intelligent, too. The girls here have to speak at least two other languages."

"Including Russian?" asked Gaunt dryly.

"Naturally." Brozman stroked a hand over his close-cropped grey hair and gave the same wisp of a smile. "The management are realists." Abruptly he changed the subject. "I believe you left the Trade Fair after lunch. How did you spend your afternoon?"

"Sightseeing." Gaunt met the question calmly. "Here and there around the city."

"Including the castle?"

"For a spell."

Brozman pursed his lips. "There was an incident of some kind—the reports are vague. Did you notice anything?"

"No." Gaunt shook his head.

"We have no real witnesses." Brozman turned to Maggie Dimond and sighed. "So—both of you were there, but neither can help. A pity."

"But not your worry," suggested Gaunt.

"No. It was only a scuffle." Brozman paused as their drinks arrived, then sent the hostess on her way with a friendly slap on the rump. He switched his attention to Carol. "While you and I had to spend our day at the Trade Fair, eh? Did you like what we have on offer, Miss Marek? Perhaps place some orders?"

"I don't work for a major-league company." Carol took a sip from her glass then shrugged. "As much as anything, we want to know what the opposition has to offer."

"But you buy a little," murmured Brozman. "Then next year, perhaps a little more—and so we establish a pattern. Do you have bears in Scotland?"

"Bears?" She blinked at him.

"The large, brown, angry, four-footed kind," said Brozman solemnly. He glanced at Maggie Dimond.

"In zoos, yes." She frowned at Gaunt for help.

"And at football," murmured Gaunt. "We call them spectators."

Brozman chuckled. "Our bears roam wild, in the mountain country to the east. Hunting is controlled, of course—but tourists who want a trophy pay a lot of money for the privilege."

"And there's a connection?" asked Gaunt.

Brozman nodded seriously. "The game-wardens know the bear colonies and their habits. They will choose a bear which would make a good trophy, entice it by leaving food, then establish a habit pattern for the animal by leaving more food at the same place at the same time each day."

"Then along comes the hunter with his rifle? You lay it on for him."

"It's called sport," said Brozman cynically. "But the important thing is to establish the habit, for the pattern to be accepted." He gestured apologetically. "We don't see our foreign buyers as animals, but—"

"But if they get into the habit of placing orders, fine?" Carol eyed him frostily. "I don't intend being anyone's trophy, Colonel."

"Neither do the bears," said Brozman. "It just happens."

They finished their drinks, and Brozman insisted on ordering another round. Then, a little later, their hostess came over and spoke to him briefly. Brozman nodded, then, as she turned to go, he rose to his feet.

"A telephone call," he said apologetically. "My people usually know where to find me. I'll only be a minute."

He left, following the girl, and Maggie Dimond immediately leaned across the table.

"Thank you for coming," she told Gaunt. "I—I wanted everything to seem normal." She touched Carol's arm apologetically. "And I used you. I'm sorry."

"There's always a first time." There was no particular animosity in Carol's voice. "But I learn fast."

The older woman nodded.

"Stepan spoke to you?" she asked Gaunt.

"And made me an offer," said Gaunt.

She understood. "He thought it was worth a try."

"You didn't?"

"No." She gave a small, bitter smile. "That's meant as a compliment."

Gaunt sighed. "Maggie, what the hell are you into? Maybe you're the one who should be on that plane tomorrow."

"Since this afternoon, I've thought about that." Maggie Dimond was serious. She lowered her voice, a new urgency in her words. "I'm frightened now—I'll admit it. But in a way I started all this." She glanced at Carol. "You told me your father is Czech."

"Was, is—" Carol shrugged, and waited.

"Then you might understand even better than I do," said Maggie Dimond wearily. "Stepan Valachova isn't a criminal. Not by my standards."

"Would Brozman see it that way?" demanded Gaunt.

"No. He'd probably brand him more dangerous than a plain, vicious criminal like Matthew Garr." She stared down at her glass for a moment. "But I can't tell you why. I'm sorry."

"Maybe that makes two of us," said Gaunt. He saw Brozman coming back towards them. "How about right now? Do you want us to stay?"

"No." Her head came up and suddenly an amused glint was back in her eyes. "When you get down to basics, he's just a man, isn't he?"

Gaunt couldn't think of an answer to that.

Brozman joined them again. He was smiling from ear to ear.

"You know an Englishman named Alford?"

Gaunt nodded.

"He was arrested for creating a disturbance—it appears he accused a German visitor of making indecent advances to his wife. I told the sergeant handling the case to take another look at Mrs. Alford, that it was an obvious misunderstanding." The smile became a chuckle. "Or the German was drunk."

"I'll quote you." Gaunt grinned. "What's your real job, Colonel? Security?"

"Security?" Brozman's eyes narrowed. "Why?"

"Whatever you want, it seems to happen," said Gaunt. He shook his head, playing the envious stranger. "In my job, when I say jump, nobody moves a muscle. You—well, you carry a lot of weight."

"A little." Brozman relaxed and gave a vague dismissive gesture. "My government places considerable importance on visitors' welfare. We want everything to go smoothly, Mr. Gaunt. Then, when you go home, when you submit your report to your special committee—"

"They'll probably read, file, and forget, believe me." Gaunt made a gloomy business of glancing at his watch. "Anyway, thanks for the drinks."

"It's time we moved on," nodded Carol, taking her cue.

Brozman made only a token protest. As they left, he shifted closer to Maggie Dimond and signalled the hostess to refill their glasses.

Outside the night sky was bright with stars and the air was frosty. Turning up her coat collar, Carol shivered a little then took Gaunt's arm.

"Cold?" asked Gaunt.

"No. More glad to get out of there." She looked at him, puzzled. "What were you trying to do?"

"With Brozman?" Gaunt shrugged. "I want to keep him happy about me, just as long as I can." He paused as they reached Vaclav Square, the statue of King Wenceslaus a bold silhouette in the starlight. "Do we find a taxi, or walk?"

"Let's walk," she decided.

They did, taking their time, the city's streets once again quiet and almost deserted. Above their heads the dark outlines of the inevitable flags and propaganda banners hung like limp, lifeless shadows. Only an occasional vehicle went past, headlamp beams stabbing the night.

It was an eery experience. A patrol of two militiamen ambled along the pavement and passed them, rifles slung, one smoking a cigarette. Gaunt felt Carol's grip on his arm tighten for a moment, then relax again. He didn't imagine any Czech would have reacted that way. To them, patrols were probably just part of the scenery.

It took about ten minutes before they saw the tall outline of the Smetana Hotel ahead. A moment later, Carol made a deliberate business of stopping to look into a brightly lit shop window where a collection of ceramic figures were displayed under a notice "For Export Buyers."

"Jonny." She turned and faced him. "Can I ask you something?"

"Go ahead," he invited.

"It's personal." She hesitated. "It was last night, when I told you Eric Garfield's wife was pregnant. You—well, it was the way you reacted."

"What about it?" he asked warily.

"Like someone had kicked you." Carol paused uncertainly, then looked at him carefully. "Was there a reason? If you can tell me, I'd like to know."

"It's no particular secret." Gaunt smiled at her wryly. In the light from the shop window her face was serious. "I'm divorced. We used to be married." He kept the smile on his lips. "Eric Garfield made her happy again. He should make a pretty good parent."

"I see." She let Gaunt nudge her away from the shop window and they resumed walking. "I shouldn't have asked."

"Maybe I'm glad you did." He meant it.

The hotel lobby was quiet when they went in. At the reception desk, a clerk yawned as he gave them their room keys then wished them good night. They took the elevator up to the eighth floor and went along the carpeted corridor to Carol's door.

"Home again." She said it in a quiet voice, used her key to open the door, then looked up at him. "I think I'd better say good night."

It seemed totally natural and inevitable that he took her in his arms and their lips met. Gaunt tried to fight a tide of need and longing as he held the dark-haired girl close.

Gently, reluctantly, she pushed away.

"Good night, Jonny," she said huskily.

She went into her room and closed the door.

Slowly, Gaunt walked along to his own room. Once inside, he tossed his sheepskin and jacket on a chair, loosened his tie, and lit a cigarette.

He felt more restless and unsettled than he had for a long time. The bedside bar had been restocked and he poured himself a beer then tried the TV set. One channel was finished for the night, the other was showing an ice hockey match.

He watched the play for a spell. Tiring of it, he switched off, went over to the window, opened the curtains and looked out.

The bridge over the river was empty of traffic. A thin crescent moon had appeared and was shining down on the high-pitched roofs and turrets of the old city. It looked a cool, peaceful, innocent world.

He stood there for a long time. A town clock somewhere began striking a mellow double-beat chime. As it ended, another bell began, distant and fainter.

Gaunt smoked another cigarette at the window, more for something to do than because he wanted it. He had stubbed it out and was turning away when he heard a light tap on the room door. He heard it again, went over, and opened the door.

"Just me," said Carol Marek. She wore her white robe, her dark hair was tied back by a ribbon, and her feet were in slippers. "I've got a problem."

"Come in." He closed the door again once she'd entered. "Like what?"

"Maggie Dimond. She's back, the wall between us is thin, and Brozman's with her." She gave a mock grimace. "They're having a noisy time. When I left, he was singing." She paused, and smiled almost shyly at him. "Could you give a girl a bed for the night?"

"Why not?" said Gaunt quietly. "It's lonely on your own."

They looked at each other for a long moment. Then she stood calmly while he undid the ribbon in her hair.

"Wait." She reached out, touched the light switch beside the door, and the room became shadows in the dim glow of moonlight.

Their lips met, gently at first, exploring, then with a gradual, growing urgency.

"Jonny." She guided his hands down to the tie-belt of her robe.

She said his name again, just once, softly, and her arms went around him.

Jonathan Gaunt woke early but slowly the next morning. He lay quietly for a few minutes, listening to the gentle, regular breathing of the dark-haired girl still sleeping peacefully beside him. Moving carefully, not wanting to disturb her, he got out of bed, splashed some water on his face then, not bothering to shave, dressed quickly.

Carol was still asleep. He went back and looked down at her. Bending over her, he kissed her lightly on the forehead. She didn't stir.

Picking up his sheepskin, he tiptoed to the door, went out, and closed the door gently again behind him. Then, pulling on the sheepskin, he headed for the elevator.

Janos Barta had said breakfast at eight. Walking briskly in streets busy with people journeying to work, Gaunt made his way to the Old Town Square. From there, he reached the side-street café and was still a few minutes early as he sat at a table and ordered coffee.

A middle-aged waitress in a greasy overall shuffled over and dumped a basin-sized cup in front of him. He paid, nodded his thanks, poured in some sugar, then stirred the coffee and sat back for a moment, watching the black liquid swirl and steam.

He felt happy, free of tension, more positive about what he was doing than he had for some time. Rubbing a thumb along his unshaven chin, he gave a half-smile.

Whatever kind of news Barta might bring, whatever the reality ahead, he felt ready to cope.

Two more cups of coffee and almost forty minutes later, he wasn't so sure. There was still no sign of Barta. Other customers had entered and left the café, men and women in work-clothes, a policeman who was an obvious regular.

But no Janos Barta. Gaunt chewed his lip, glanced at his watch yet again, and decided he'd wait the full hour, no more.

The waitress was hovering. He shook his head and she shrugged and turned away. The café door swung open again, letting in a draught of cold air, and he stared as Carol Marek came in. Her face was pale, almost as pale as the white wool of her Icelandic jacket. Seeing him, she came straight over.

"Something's happened, Jonny," she said huskily and urgently. "It's bad."

"Barta?"

She nodded. "There's someone waiting outside."

He rose and followed her out. Janos Barta's battered old Skoda taxi was parked across the street but the driver was a fair-haired boy who didn't look old enough to hold a driving licence. Seeing them, the boy gave Carol a quick inquiring glance and showed his relief when she gave a reassuring gesture.

Gaunt followed her over and they got into the rear seat. A threadbare travelling rug had been draped over the front seats. It had a dark red staining which had seeped through in several places.

The fair-haired boy muttered to Carol then set the Skoda moving. He wasn't a particularly good driver, but he was in a hurry.

"How much do you know?" asked Gaunt as they began travelling.

"Only the basics, Jonny." Carol gestured helplessly. "Janos Barta has been shot, badly wounded." She nodded towards their driver. "His name is Walter. He's taking us to him. They found the taxi in the street just outside his apartment about six this morning, with Barta unconscious in the front seat."

"He got there on his own?" asked Gaunt.

"It seems that way." She bit her lip. "They got him into his apartment—he lives with his sister. Then they got a doctor." She broke off, spoke briefly to the boy, and he answered without taking his eyes from the road. Then she turned to Gaunt again. "The doctor is someone they can trust. Barta came round, said he had to speak to you, and Walter was sent—that's all he knows."

"Then what?"

"Walter came to the Smetana and asked for you. They rang your room." She looked at him wryly for a moment. "I answered. I got him to tell me a little, and I remembered you were to meet Barta for breakfast. Walter reckoned that would be at the café."

Gaunt nodded a weary understanding.

"I told him," he said bitterly. "I told him to stay clear of trouble." He hardly noticed the way the Skoda lurched as it took a massive pot-hole without slowing. "What are his chances?"

"I don't know. He could be dying, or it sounds that way. The other thing is, he'd been badly beaten—that must have been before he was shot." She put a hand on his arm. "I'm sorry, Jonny."

Gaunt didn't answer. He was thinking of Barta, of how the middle-aged Czech had warned him and urged him to get out. Now, it was tragic irony that Barta should pay the penalty for his having ignored it.

He felt sick with a cold anger which brought him close to trembling. Maggie Dimond and the man Valachova, Matthew Garr and his hired thugs—the whole mad circus of violence, Colonel Brozman in the middle like a sleeping ring-master, had to be stopped. Whatever that took.

The fair-haired youngster drove them south-east, into a down-at-heel area of the city where no flags flew and shabby buildings lined old, narrow streets. The Skoda stopped at the kerb outside a crumbling tenement block. As it did, a girl in a leather jacket appeared at the tenement's entrance. She nodded to their driver then stepped back into shelter again.

Glancing round at his passengers, Walter signalled them out and opened his own door.

"Hold on," said Gaunt.

Pushing a hand down between the squabs of the rear seat, he found the hard bulk of the automatic pistol he'd left there after the incident at the castle. Bringing the gun out, he tucked it into his waistband, then met Carol's gaze.

"Ready," he said quietly. "Let's go."

They followed Walter into the tenement, past the girl on sentry duty. The youngster led them up three flights of dark, gloomy stairs and tapped on one of the doors on a landing. The door opened. Another young man beckoned them in.

The door closed behind them. Still leading the way, Walter brought them through a small hallway into a shabby living-room. A framed photograph met their eyes from the opposite wall. It showed a younger Barta, smiling and confident, in academic robes.

"That was many years ago, Mr. Gaunt," said a sad, quiet voice behind them.

They turned. A middle-aged woman, grey-haired, her face pale, shock in her eyes, looked at them gravely.

"I am Anna Barta—Janos's sister." Her English was slow but precise, as if she hadn't used the language for some time. "Thank you for coming."

"How is he?" asked Gaunt.

"Dying, Mr. Gaunt." There was resignation in her voice. "We dare not take him to a hospital. Other people might—well, suffer. You understand?"

Tight-lipped, Gaunt nodded.

"Even if we did, it would be hopeless." She drew a deep breath. "A good friend who is a doctor is with him. Please do not ask his name."

She signalled them to follow her and they went back across the little hallway.

Janos Barta was lying on a bed in a small, plainly furnished room.

His face was a grey, putty colour and livid with bruising. He had been stripped to the waist and thick, blood-soaked pads of dressings had been taped to his body, where more livid bruising was visible.

Two other people were already in the room. A dark-haired man, in his thirties, was packing instruments back into a medical bag. A woman, younger, good-looking, dressed in a skirt and sweater, was bathing the worst of the bruising on Barta's face with the deft touch of a professional nurse.

Both stood back. The dark-haired doctor looked at Anna Barta and shook his head.

"Jonathan." Barta's voice was little more than a whisper. One hand made a fractional movement, beckoning him over.

The doctor saw the question in Gaunt's eyes and shrugged. He signalled the nurse, and they went out of the room. Anna Barta stayed in the doorway with Carol, silent but watchful.

"This time, I was not very clever." Barta forced the semblance of a smile as Gaunt bent over him. His voice was low and halting. "Sorry."

"What happened, Janos?" asked Gaunt. He laid a hand on Barta's shoulder. "Who did it?"

"Garr—Garr and his men." Barta tried to move, gave a quick grimace of pain, and slumped back again. "I was a fool, Jonathan." He paused, struggling for breath. "It was last night, when I went back to the *autokemp*. I—I must have asked too many questions. They grabbed me outside, took me to their chalet."

"And did this?" Gaunt looked at the bruising, saw the way Barta's lips were gashed and one eye swollen until it was almost closed.

"They were—very forceful." Barta coughed. A small rivulet of blood trickled from the corner of his mouth. "I told them a little. That you'd hired me to watch them but that I knew nothing else." He managed to grin again. "Then I pretended to faint—at least, I think I pretended. They left me alone for a minute, and I got out a window, but not quietly enough. They came after me, into the trees."

"Who shot you?"

Barta gave a slight head-shake. "I don't know, Jonathan. I—I got to some bushes and hid. Then I fainted for real. The next thing I knew they were gone and something wild and furry was sniffing at my face." He struggled for breath again. "So I—I got to where I'd left the taxi and—and just drove home. But you can forget about the *autokemp*. They'll be far away by now."

"It doesn't matter." Gaunt pursed his lips, knowing Barta was right, and filled with a total admiration for the courage behind the simply told story. "You made it back, Janos."

"I feel cold," said Barta suddenly. He sounded puzzled. "Is it cold?"

"Yes," lied Gaunt.

"Interesting." Barta looked up at him calmly. "But I am fairly—yes, fairly certain I am dying." Fresh blood bubbled from his lips and he coughed again. "I want you to promise me something, Jonathan."

"Name it," said Gaunt quietly.

"My young people." Barta struggled for another rasping breath. "Don't get them involved. They may want to help but—"

"I'll keep them out of it," Gaunt said. "Rely on that."

"Good." Barta smiled at him. "They—they matter. Maybe for tomorrow or the next day, eh?"

"They matter."

"One other thing—" Barta struggled to go on. "Watch Colonel Brozman. He waits, then—then when he does act—"

"I'll remember," promised Gaunt.

"Watch Brozman," repeated Barta, the words fading to a murmur. He sighed, a harsh, rasping sound, then his eyes closed and his head lolled against the pillow.

He was still breathing, faintly and irregularly. Gaunt stood back.

"I'll stay with him," said Anna Barta.

She came over, knelt beside her brother, and took one of his hands between her own. There were tears in her eyes.

Gaunt felt a touch on his arm. Beckoning, Carol led him out of the room. They went through to the living-room, where the doctor and nurse were standing drinking coffee. Walter and the other student were sitting over by the window, just waiting.

"Mr. Gaunt." The dark-haired doctor greeted him with a slight nod, then gestured towards the coffee-pot.

"No, thanks." Gaunt brought out his cigarettes and lit one. He drew on it deeply, then asked, "There's no chance?"

"None." The doctor's voice was flat and positive. "Janos Barta is what you would call a tough old bird, Mr. Gaunt. He should have been dead before he got here. But—no." He shook his head. "I think one thing has kept him alive, and that was waiting for you."

"But if you moved him—" began Carol.

"He has two bullet wounds," said the doctor wearily. "The one that matters least tore a lung. The other—all I can say is it penetrated the rib cage then glanced off bone." He switched his gaze to Gaunt. "Have you any idea what a bullet can do when it travels at random inside a man's chest?"

"A mess," said Gaunt quietly.

"So whether we move him or not, he will die," said the Czech. He hesitated. "There is another reason. At a hospital, there would be questions, the police, then the STB. Too many people would be put at risk, Mr. Gaunt."

"You took the risk of coming here," reminded Carol. "Why?"

The man shaped a shrug. "Years ago, when he was Professor Barta, I was one of his students. Now—well, there are plenty like me. I am not an activist, maybe not even a dissident. But—" He left it there.

"He taught you pretty well," said Gaunt.

That brought a slight twist of a smile. Gaunt left it at that and doctor and nurse began a low-voiced conversation.

"Had Maggie Dimond any plans for this morning?" he asked Carol.

"None I know about." She glanced at her wrist-watch. "She should still be at the hotel."

"Will you go there and find her?"

Carol looked at him carefully and nodded. "If that's what you want."

"It is." Gaunt had taken his own decision. "Tell her either I talk face-to-face with Stepan Valachova this morning or Colonel Brozman gets everything I know."

"Will she believe it?"

"She will, if you tell her I can be on the next plane out of Prague," said Gaunt stonily. "Then I'd make a phone call the moment I was over in the West."

"That might be a good idea, for real," said Carol. She pursed her lips for a moment. "All right, I won't argue. I'll ask Walter to drive me over."

"Don't let him get involved beyond that," said Gaunt sharply, Barta's words still in the forefront of his mind. "And warn Maggie Dimond that Garr is still somewhere out there. Whatever she sets up, it has to be foolproof."

"Garr-proof. Not to mention a certain colonel," she said. "You're staying here?"

"Yes."

Carol went over and talked to the fair-haired youngster. Slowly, almost reluctantly, Walter got to his feet and followed her out of the room. The main door of the apartment clicked open and banged shut again. Then a minute or so later Gaunt heard the old Skoda taxi start up and drive away.

A faint, almost apologetic throat-clearing sound made him turn. The nurse stood beside him, a fresh mug of coffee in her hands. She offered it with a smile which was a mixture of understanding and sympathy.

"Thank you." He took it from her, and she murmured something in Czech then left him alone.

The coffee was black, strong, and scalding hot. But even just holding it gave him something to do.

Twenty minutes passed. There was a low call from the bedroom. Doctor and nurse hurried through, then, after a pause, Anna Barta came in.

"It's over," she said quietly.

The young student still sitting near the window buried his head in his hands. Barta's sister went over to comfort him.

Gaunt left them and went through to the bedroom. A clean sheet had been drawn over Janos Barta's body and the doctor was snapping shut his medical bag. Handing the bag to the nurse, he signalled her to leave them.

"We will arrange things," he told Gaunt as the door closed. "The death certificate will say natural causes—a heart attack. There are people we can trust for the other arrangements." He considered the threadbare carpet for a moment. "That way, we will have no difficulties, no problems."

Gaunt nodded. "What about his sister? If she needs help—"

"Thank you, but no." The doctor shook his head firmly. "We can take care of everything, Mr. Gaunt."

Turning, Gaunt went through to the living-room again. The young student had gone. There were others to be told.

A lot of people were going to mourn Janos Barta's death. Standing there, Gaunt felt the weight of the gun in his waistband and his mouth tightened.

That part was an ending. The rest was about to begin.

It was another half hour before Carol Marek returned. By then, Gaunt had had enough of the atmosphere of sadness in the third-floor apartment. He was standing in the tenement building's doorway when the old Skoda taxi turned into the street and halted beside him with a protesting squeal of worn-out brake-shoes.

Crossing the pavement, he opened the rear passenger door and got in.

"It's fixed," said Carol as he settled beside her and closed the door again. "She didn't like it, but it's fixed. She's on her way to join Valachova, and they'll be waiting for us." Then she took another look at his face and her manner changed. "Barta?"

"Yes."

Walter swung round in the driver's seat and stared at him, his young face a tight mask of disbelief. Turning to Carol, he spoke quickly and angrily.

"He says he wants to help," translated Carol with a frown. "He says there are plenty like him—they'll all help, any way you want."

"No." Gaunt shook his head firmly. "Tell him Barta didn't want that. Tell him I made a promise."

She did, beating down a new protest from the fair-haired youngster. At last, reluctantly, he gave an unhappy nod.

"Right," said Gaunt with some relief. "Back to Maggie Dimond. You're sure she contacted Valachova?"

"Yes. I was with her when she telephoned him." She saw Gaunt's raised eyebrow and gave a slight smile. "Don't worry. She used a pay phone in the hotel lobby."

"And the meeting?"

"A museum and library of some kind—I've got the address and directions. It's about thirty kilometres out of the city." Carol hesitated and frowned. "You'll need transport. If you don't want to use Walter—"

"I can hire, self-drive." He had another, more pressing problem. "You said she was on her way. Any chance she was followed?"

"I wondered when you'd ask," Carol said dryly. "Someone tried it —or it looked that way."

"In a blue Polski-Fiat?"

She nodded. "Maggie took a taxi. I got Walter to tail her, just in case. We spotted the blue car, then—well, we made a splendid job of stalling the engine, blocking everything at traffic lights. She's clear."

"Good." Another major worry had been removed. "No trouble afterwards?"

"Not particularly." She eyed him innocently. "Just a few words I'd never heard put together before. Shouldn't we get started?"

"We?" He frowned. "What about that Trade Fair?"

"We," she repeated firmly. "Who's going to miss me for a few hours?"

They had Walter take them one last journey, back into the city to the main Cedok state travel bureau, and said goodbye to him outside. He clasped each of them by the hand, showed a quick indignation when Gaunt tried to pay him, then the little taxi rasped away and merged into the other traffic.

Inside the bureau, the routine was smooth once Gaunt produced his passport and a clerk had checked his visa. There was a choice between a Russian-built Lada station wagon and the locally produced Skoda range.

He chose the Skoda. There were more of them around. In ten minutes it was delivered outside, a rear-engined coupe, black in colour, with low mileage and a full fuel tank. He paid the deposit, collected a tourist road-map, and thanked the clerk.

They were on their way.

Their road lay west, over the river, then joining the Plzenska through route. Traffic began to thin as they left the city behind and the first green fields took the place of buildings. Further on they passed a few small lakes and Carol began frowning between the Cedok map and a slip of paper with written directions she'd produced from her handbag.

Exactly on twenty-two kilometres they turned off the through route. From there, they travelled on minor roads through farming country. Traffic was reduced to an occasional tractor or horse and cart.

"Next on your right," said Carol at last, as the Skoda purred through a small village. "Yes. There—at the sign."

Two old stone gateposts marked the start of a gravelled driveway lined by tall, thick bushes. The bushes seemed to go on for a long time then, suddenly, they emerged in the open. Ahead of them lay an imposing pink-stoned building, part mansion and part medieval castle. It had turrets and arrow-slit windows, a central courtyard area with a hint of Italian about its architecture, and a wide scatter of outbuildings.

But two large, empty tour buses sat incongruously on a reasonably new tarmac area beside the main door. There were litter bins, more signs, and the arch above the centre block had been topped by a giant red star made from plywood. It still was cold enough for an edging of white frost to be visible on the red.

"This place?" Gaunt slowed the Skoda to a crawl and grunted in surprise. "You're sure?"

"Positive. We're in the stately homes league, East European style. They were taken over, then nobody knew what to do with the damned things." Carol grimaced. "Some of the top Party people took a few. Some are used as week-end hideaways for visiting VIP's. But the rest are Houses of Culture. This one is called Prodanov House."

They parked the Skoda beside the tour buses, got out, and walked up the stone steps which led into the building. A turnstile gate greeted them at the main door, and clicked as they pushed through it. On the far side, an elderly woman wrapped in a heavy coat sat reading a magazine. She looked up long enough to give them a cursory glance and a nod, then went back to reading again.

A carpeted, roped-off corridor funnelled them from there through a large draughty hall which had stone walls and a high, vaulted ceiling. Framed maps and old oil paintings flanked them on either side. They heard a growing buzz of voices, then arrived in a vast, circular area which had a domed roof.

The voices were schoolchildren, a small horde of them being given an escorted tour around a display of exhibits. They ranged from an old, highly polished stage-coach to what looked like a history of agricultural machinery through the ages.

Taking Carol's arm, Gaunt looked around. There was an upper

gallery, lined with books, deserted. He noticed some of the children had found their way into the stage-coach.

"What now?" asked Carol, puzzled.

"Wait." He looked up at the gallery again. A door had opened. A bearded figure emerged, came over to the gallery rail, leaned on it, then gave a nod in their direction.

They stayed where they were while Stepan Valachova came down a flight of stairs and walked towards them. He seemed less confident and relaxed than the last time Gaunt had seen him, but his manner was still cool and controlled as he greeted them. He was wearing the same sports suit, with a white shirt and a dark wine-coloured tie.

"My apologies for not meeting you when you arrived." There was a sardonic edge behind the words, and Valachova thumbed over his shoulder towards the gallery. "From up there, I have a good view down to the road. It seemed a good idea to make sure you were on your own."

"So now you know," said Gaunt woodenly. "Where's Maggie Dimond?"

"Waiting on us." Valachova pursed his lips briefly. "Your friend the taxi-driver—?"

"He died," said Carol. "Were you expecting a miracle?"

"No." Valachova's lips shaped a faint, humourless smile. "Miracles have been in short supply in this country for some time." He drew a deep breath. "It's chilly here. Heating is kept at an economic minimum. Let me take you somewhere warmer."

They let him lead the way, down a side-corridor past more paintings and sculptures. Beyond that, going through a doorway, they entered a small room laid out as a portrait gallery.

"My ancestors," said Valachova dryly. He paused, considering the wigged, aristocratic figures, women in court dress, men portrayed with a sword at their side or in some studied, thoughtful pose. "The Valachova family is old in Bohemia, Mr. Gaunt. This was their home, my father was a count. Now, I'm caretaker and the rest is a museum. Odd."

"I wouldn't know," said Gaunt. "I'm from a long line of peasants."

"Scottish peasants—yes, Mr. Gaunt, it happens I know all about them." Valachova stood where he was and looked at him strangely.

"This ridiculously titled Queen's and Lord Treasurer's Remembrancer you work for—does that mean some degree of personal loyalty to your Queen Elizabeth?"

Gaunt shrugged. "She pays my wages."

"The question embarrasses you?" Valachova produced a key from his pocket and unlocked another door. Then he looked round again. "Your Queen Elizabeth, of course, is of the House of Hanover. They have held the British throne for generations. But before them, of course, you had the Stuart kings." He glanced at Carol and gave a slight, quizzical smile. "History can be an intriguing subject, Miss Marek."

"If you say so." Carol showed her impatience. "That's not why we're here."

"Wrong," said Valachova quietly. "For instance, your friend's Scottish peasant ancestors fought a battle at a place called Culloden. They lost. But if they had won, we might not be meeting."

"Meaning?" She frowned.

"I claim direct descent from the Royal House of Stuart." Valachova met Gaunt's incredulous stare and nodded. "But for Culloden, I might conceivably be King Stepan the First of Great Britain. Intriguing, isn't it?"

He opened the door and gestured them through.

CHAPTER 7

The flight of steps was old and worn, a tight spiral climbing between damp walls of rough-hewn stone. It was a long climb. At the top, another door opened at a touch and they walked into a large room laid out as a mixture of study and studio. A turret window gave a view across fields and countryside. The wooden floor was bare apart from a few threadbare rugs. But the room was warm, its heat coming from a log fire which smoked and crackled in a stone hearth.

Maggie Dimond was standing at the turret window. She wore a doubleknit sweater and cord trousers, her hair caught back at the nape of her neck by a plain ivory clasp.

"The man died," Valachova told her as he came in last and closed the door behind him. He shrugged and moved over to stand beside the fire. "It makes things worse, of course. Worse all round."

Maggie Dimond said nothing for a moment. She greeted Carol with a fractional nod then focussed her attention on Gaunt.

"You're a fool, Jonathan," she said in a voice which held tired hostility. "But you wanted this meeting and we're here." She glanced at Carol again, then added angrily, "Your message didn't give us much option, did it?"

"I meant it that way." Gaunt considered the room, its comfortable, well-worn furniture, the artist's easel near the window, and the long, unpolished table covered with small pots of paint and scattered pieces of pottery, some plain, some partially decorated. He turned to Valachova. "You live here?"

"The authorities allowed me to stay, as resident caretaker." Valachova gave a humourless smile. "At least I don't have to pay rent. I have another job, my real work—I design ceramic ware." He paused then said doggedly, "Mr. Gaunt, last night I made you an offer. It's still open. I—yes, I might be able to improve on it."

"That's not why I'm here," said Gaunt.

Valachova sighed resignedly. "Then what do you want?"

"The truth. Exactly what's going on and why."

"I see." Valachova stared down at his hands. "And if we refuse? You would really contact Colonel Brozman?"

"You decide that," said Gaunt.

Maggie Dimond scowled at him. "Maybe you wouldn't believe us."

"Try me," suggested Gaunt, turning towards her. Then, out of the corner of his eye, he saw Valachova taking a sidling step towards the table. Saying nothing, he quietly drew the Luger pistol from his waistband.

"Please." Valachova raised his hands in a quick, almost comical gesture. Moving carefully, he picked up a small ball of modelling clay from the table, looked towards Carol as if seeking sympathy, then fingered the clay with slow deliberation. "I'm sorry. Sometimes I need a little help when I'm thinking. I've another question, Mr. Gaunt. If we give you what you want, how will you use it?"

Gaunt shrugged, and tucked the Luger out of sight again. "That wouldn't be your worry. You might even benefit."

"Matthew Garr," said Valachova shrewdly. He played with the modelling clay again. "You have a score to settle there. It would be logical enough to consider using us as some form of bait. Am I right?"

"Perhaps," said Gaunt. "It happens the man who died this morning was a friend of mine."

"Yes." The word came from Valachova like a sigh. "Your friend— what was his name?"

Gaunt shook his head. "Maybe I can't remember."

"To protect other people, some dissident group?" Valachova waited for an answer. When he didn't get one, he shook his head philosophically. "Yes, I understand. Perhaps we've no quarrel at all, Mr. Gaunt." He paused, glanced at Maggie Dimond, and smiled as she gave a fractional nod. "For a start, suppose we sit down?"

Abandoning the pottery clay, Valachova placed chairs around the fireplace and set some fresh logs in position. Then, settling like the others, he sat for a moment just watching the sparking, smoking wood.

"How well do you know British history?" he asked suddenly.

Gaunt blinked. "Only what I was taught at school."

"Miss Marek?"

Carol shook her head. "I learned a few dates. It wasn't my favourite subject."

"A pity," mused Valachova. "Still, both of you may remember that James the Second was the last of the Stuart kings of England. That eventually he became so unpopular he had to flee to France."

"That much, yes." Gaunt nodded, puzzled.

"It happened in 1688," murmured Maggie Dimond. "He escaped by boat with his queen, their infant son, and not much else." She saw Valachova's expression. "I'm sorry, Stepan. You tell it."

"This part, eh?" Valachova grinned at her. "All right. In England, the new king was William of Orange. Later, the succession went to Queen Anne and she was followed by the first of the Hanoverians. But a lot of people still regarded the exiled Stuarts as the rightful rulers. In France, for instance, Louis the Fourteenth made them welcome—though that was mostly for political purposes."

"It still happens today," said Gaunt. "Rulers in exile can be useful."

"Correct." Valachova didn't mind the interruption. "And back in England—Britain, if you prefer—the Stuarts also had many supporters. They called themselves Jacobites. We might label them yesterday's dissidents."

A log toppled from the fire. Valachova got up, shoved it back in place with his foot, then sat down again. Gaunt waited, caught up in a mood of unreality. He was half a continent away from home, involved in a mystery that had already claimed three lives, yet here he was, sitting in someone's old castle, sitting and listening to what amounted to a history lesson.

"I'm sorry." Valachova seemed to sense his mood. "You want the truth, Mr. Gaunt. But to understand it, you first have to realize the background."

Speaking quietly, to no one in particular, Valachova went on. In a few brief sentences, he sketched the next section of the Stuart saga. After James the Second died, still in exile, his son proclaimed himself James the Third—and made several attempts to win back his throne.

"All ended in disaster," said Valachova. "But James did succeed in one direction. He found himself a queen. He married Princess

Maria Clementina Sobieska, a granddaughter of the King of Poland, a very well-connected young woman. Their first child was a boy who was christened Charles Edward Stuart." He smiled at Gaunt. "In time, that child became the famed Bonnie Prince Charlie who raised his standard in Scotland. He was loved by your Scottish peasants. They fought hard for his cause."

"They died for it," said Gaunt. The Highland clans had flocked to support Charles Edward Stuart in what history labeled the '45 Rebellion. Their sole reward had been to perish in the mud under English bayonets. "They died—he ran."

"But what happened to him after that?" persisted Valachova. "How did he live, where did he go?"

Gaunt shook his head. It was enough for most Scots to remember the '45 as the end of the Highland clans, the start of an aftermath of sorrow which had crippled half a country. Cleared from their homes, thousands of families had eventually been forced to leave Scotland. Crammed aboard leaking ships, they'd only known they were bound for some place called America.

"Charles Stuart became a wanderer," declared Valachova. He scratched his beard for a moment, a man thinking aloud. "It couldn't have been easy, to have suddenly become an embarrassment wherever he went. For the rest of his life it stayed that way. When he died, he had degenerated into a fat, moody drunkard whose wife preferred to share her bed with an obscure poet. There were no children of the marriage. His claim to the English throne passed to his brother Henry, who was a priest."

"Wait." Carol frowned at him. "Downstairs, when you met us, you said—"

"That I might have been King Stepan?" Valachova chuckled and looked slightly embarrassed. "Perhaps I exaggerated a little. But—yes, I claim Charles Edward Stuart as an ancestor. You see, when he was wandering around Europe he was a guest of many titled families. He visited here more than once, became attracted to a daughter of the Valachova family—and fathered an illegitimate son in the process. So my claim would be on what I think is called the 'wrong side of the blanket.'"

"Any others like you around?" asked Gaunt.

"The recognized claimants, legitimate but less direct, are a Bavarian family," said Valachova. "Still, what I've told you is true. My family were rather proud of what happened and kept some relics of those visits." He glanced at Maggie Dimond and smiled wryly. "But we're up to date now—to the time when Mrs. Dimond first came to see me, unannounced and unexpected."

"Two years ago," said Maggie Dimond. "It was my first visit to Prague."

"How did you meet?" asked Carol, openly curious.

"Chance." Maggie Dimond showed she wouldn't be hurried but her tone was no longer hostile. "For the first time in my life I had money and I wanted a break. I came on holiday, and I've always been interested in history—"

"At honours level," murmured Gaunt.

"Yes. So I'd read a little about Czech history. When I came out, I thought it would be interesting to find out more about that Queen of Bohemia who came from Scotland."

"The one Colonel Brozman mentioned?" asked Carol.

"The same," agreed Maggie Dimond. "From a much earlier time. When I got to Prague, I was told the best library for records about her was here." She paused and shrugged. "So I came, met Stepan, and he told me his story about the Stuarts. I didn't particularly believe him—not at first, anyway."

"But you did by the second visit," reminded Valachova mildly. "A lot of things changed then, eh?"

"That's true." She looked at Gaunt. "When I got home after that first visit I did more reading. I decided that this man Valachova I'd met could have been genuine. So, as soon as I'd more leave due, I went out to Prague again. I took a present with me for Stepan, something I'd found in an Edinburgh junk-shop. It was a copy of an old Jacobite plate."

"And when I saw it, when she explained what it was, I nearly fainted," said Valachova frankly. "I had one like it, a plate my family had kept for generations. Yet in all that time—" He stopped. "Should I show them?"

Maggie Dimond nodded. Getting to his feet, Valachova crossed the room, opened a cupboard, and brought out two large china platters. He laid them side by side on the table then went back to the cupboard and returned with a plain glass decanter filled with a clear liquid.

"Ordinary water," he explained. "Come here, please."

They rose and joined him. The two plates were decorated with ugly, broken patterns of coloured daubs and lines, each totally unattractive, both obviously old.

"Now." Slowly, carefully, Valachova placed the glass decanter exactly in the centre of the first plate, released his grip, and stood back.

Carol gasped. Gaunt stared, taken by surprise.

As if from nowhere, trapped inside the water like some ghost from the past, the figure of a young man in Highland dress had become visible. Bonnie Prince Charlie smiled out at the world in the way which had made him the romantic centre-piece of so many legends, songs and ballads.

"The technique is called refraction painting," said Maggie Dimond, seeing their bewilderment. "The Jacobites knew the secret—the pattern on the plate uses the water in the bottle like a lens. A man's life could be at risk if he was suspected of being a supporter of the Stuarts. But he could have this, he could drink a health to 'The King over the Water'—and if there was an unexpected visitor, all he had to do was move the bottle."

She pushed the decanter slightly to one side. The image vanished.

"And I call myself an artist," said Valachova ruefully. "I design, I sketch, I paint—and I never knew. But let me show you the other plate now, Mr. Gaunt. It's one of two that your Charles Edward Stuart gave to my family, and there was a story with them. He had said as long as we kept those plates the Valachovas would hold a king's trust."

Taking the decanter again, he lowered it on the second plate. A wavering pattern showed inside the glass then came into sharper focus as he guided the decanter closer to the exact centre, then set it down.

The pattern was a map. In one corner there was a coat of arms. Along the foot, some small lettering.

"There you have the Stuart crest," said Valachova. "The wording is Latin. '*Non desideriis hominum sed voluntate Dei*—not by the desires of men but by the will of God.' The Stuart motto."

"And the map?" asked Gaunt, frowning.

"The area around this house. You see a point marked to the east?"

It was there, a small but definite cross on the shimmering outline.

"There used to be an old summer-house at that spot." Valachova leaned both hands on the table and smiled. "That same night, I went there with Mrs. Dimond. We had spades, and we dug. Then again the next night. And we found an old iron chest, Mr. Gaunt. When we opened it, it held some of the finest silver I have ever seen—plates and goblets, serving dishes and ornaments. Every last one marked with the Stuart crest."

Gaunt shaped a silent whistle of appreciation.

"That I'd have liked to see," he admitted.

"The problem was what to do with them," said Valachova. "This Socialist Democratic Republic is a greedy organization. Every last spoon would have been seized, declared the property of the State. I also have to admit that museum caretakers don't often give dinner parties."

"So you sold them?" guessed Gaunt. "Sold them in the West, through Matthew Garr?"

"Correct." Valachova nodded. "Mrs. Dimond smuggled them out in her luggage over her next two trips. I told her how to contact Garr—I knew he had already helped other friends of mine sell assets they'd got out to the West. Of course, I knew the man was a shark, a crook. But he has good contacts. Anyone selling through Garr doesn't have to worry about anything being traced back."

"How much did you get from him?" asked Gaunt.

"Two hundred thousand Swiss francs," Maggie Dimond said. "Less than a third of the price Garr probably sold at."

"It's called commission," said Gaunt sarcastically. "How about you, Maggie? How much did you clear?"

Her right hand swung hard for his face. He blocked the blow with an upraised arm, but it still hurt. Eyes blazing, she was ready to try again, but Valachova had stepped between them.

"Easy," soothed Gaunt. "You know I had to ask."

"I think you've had your answer," said Valachova. His mouth tightened. "She refused to take anything, even expenses."

"I believe it." Gaunt gave the copper-haired woman an apologetic grin and saw her anger begin to fade. He found his cigarettes and lit one. "So that's how Garr got involved." He paused, looking at Carol. She was standing beside the two plates on the table, frowning down at them. "Something wrong?"

"No. Not with these." She turned to Valachova. "But I'd like to see the other one—the second Valachova plate."

"The original?" Valachova spent a moment putting the two plates back in the cupboard. "Anyone can. It's in a display case in Prague Castle—part of a State collection. But they think it's medieval Bohemian work. That's why it was taken from here."

"So you can't get at it?"

"No. It's behind armoured glass, well guarded," said Valachova. He winked at her. "On the other hand, I am an artist—a designer. It's natural I study the past masters, for inspiration. I took five months, going along casually once a fortnight, memorizing each detail, before I could paint my own copy."

Humming to himself, he went back to the cupboard. This time the plate he produced was larger than the others, originally plain white, but wildly patterned with broken lines and whorls of colour.

The ritual with the decanter was repeated. A new map showed. It included a river and a hill, an obvious road junction and, beside the junction, a small, stylized cross.

"Look at the top," said Maggie Dimond with a strange tension in her voice.

There were two crests. One was the Stuart coat of arms, as before. The other was new, totally different.

"That's the old Royal crest of Poland." Maggie Dimond's eyes were bright with enthusiasm. "Remember that Prince Charles's mother was a Polish princess. When she married James the Third she was sixteen years old, a favourite child. Every contemporary report said her dowry was enormous."

"Jewels," said Valachova. "Pieces like the Great Ruby of Poland, which was bigger than any pigeon's egg. She brought diamonds and emeralds, even the famous Sobieska pearls, white as milk and worth a king's ransom on their own. Your Bonnie Prince Charlie inherited them, Mr. Gaunt." He moistened his lips. "Years later, we know some were sold. But only a few. The rest simply disappeared."

"You hope you've found them?" asked Gaunt.

"Yes."

So now he knew. Gaunt swallowed hard. "Suppose you're right. How much are they worth, hard cash?"

Valachova shrugged.

"Maggie?" Gaunt waited for an answer.

"All I can tell you is what the original dowry was probably worth." She was calm again, almost ice-cool, the totally efficient individual who had hacked her way up the Civil Service ladder. "I've done some research, made some calculations. If we translate every-thing into today's values, my guess would be that sixteen-year-old girl brought about six million pounds sterling in gems with her. Since then—well, about half the Sobieska jewels have never been traced." She shrugged. "Half of six million pounds is three mil-lion . . ."

Gaunt's brain felt numbed. He was still trying to believe his ears. "Why would Charles Edward bury that kind of loot and forget about it?"

There was silence in the room for a moment, silence broken only by the crackling logs on the fire. Outside, the weather had changed. The sky had greyed and there were a first few spots of rain on the window. Throwing the stub of his cigarette into the fire, Gaunt cursed inwardly. The worst part of the whole crazy story was that he almost wanted to accept it.

"The Sobieska jewels had become the Stuart nest-egg," said Mag-gie Dimond. "The English still had a price on Charles Stuart's head and there weren't too many people he could trust. And it wasn't a time when the Swiss were operating numbered bank accounts. More important, all his life until the day he died, Charles Stuart was a ro-mantic. He believed he would return home again, as king. When that happened, the Sobieska jewels could have been the first instal-ment of the royal pay-chest." She shook her head. "But there's only one way to prove it."

"Do you know where to look?" asked Gaunt.

"Yes." She gave Valachova a quick, odd glance. "Though there is a problem."

"How much does Matthew Garr know?"

"Only a little, but even that was a mistake," she admitted tiredly. "We contacted him again about a month ago. It was Stepan's idea, and I went along with it. I asked Garr if he could handle a large quantity of jewellery. But I warned him that this time we'd want a better deal and that we'd make sure of that by only feeding him one small parcel at a time."

"Just like that?" Gaunt stared at her incredulously.

"He agreed," said Valachova miserably. "We never thought—" He left it there and shook his head.

Gaunt swore softly, at no one in particular. Someone like

Matthew Garr, asked to handle a small hoard of antique silver stamped with the distinctive Stuart crest, then approached with that new proposition, could make his own research, fast—and reach his own conclusions.

But Gaunt realized he wasn't quite finished. He had to know a little more before he could think clearly, could work out any kind of plan.

"Valachova." He waited until he had the bearded man's full attention. "Suppose it all comes together. What will you do, afterwards?"

"Get out, to the West." Stepan Valachova didn't hesitate. "If one spends enough money it isn't too difficult—the easiest route is into Austria." He gestured confidently. "Then maybe a villa in the south of France, where I can become Count Valachova again. I will be a rich man, Mr. Gaunt—a very rich man."

"That's all?" Gaunt felt a vague disappointment.

"Why not?" asked Valachova cheerfully. "I have never been any kind of political animal." He raised an eyebrow in Carol's direction. "You seem annoyed, Miss Marek. Did you expect me to do something different?"

She shook her head and went over to the window to look out at the gathering drizzle of rain. Valachova shrugged.

"Maggie said you know where to look," reminded Gaunt. "You're sure?"

"Positive. I spent a lot of time studying old maps," said Valachova briskly. "The place is an old wayside shrine about twelve kilometres from here—I've been to see it. The one problem is an army post across the road from it. The troops are Russian. It's not a large unit, but—"

"It doesn't have to be," said Gaunt.

"We can do it," said Valachova.

"We?" Gaunt glanced at Maggie Dimond.

She nodded.

"I need a little help," murmured Valachova. "But this time it will be easier. We'll be better equipped."

"When?" demanded Gaunt.

"Tomorrow night." Valachova considered the burning logs in the fireplace. "First, tonight, I intend to make a final—well, survey. Then tomorrow night, with a little luck, it will be done." He gave a small, explanatory gesture. "We are allowing a safety margin. Mrs. Dimond has only a seven-day visa and tomorrow will be her fourth day."

Gaunt drew a deep breath. "Haven't you forgotten about Garr?"

"That would be difficult," admitted Valachova. He looked hopefully at Gaunt. "What are you going to do about him?"

Maggie Dimond was watching him, waiting for an answer. Over by the window, Carol looked round. She was tight-lipped, frowning, and obviously just managing to stay silent. Gaunt felt a surge of anger at the man but at the same time he knew he had only himself to blame.

"I don't know yet," he told Valachova almost curtly. He thought as he spoke. "Garr has his own problems. Most likely he's going to play a waiting game. Let him. The only way he's sure he can get to you is through Maggie." He turned to the woman. "Which means your best bet is to stay close to Colonel Brozman."

"On past form, that shouldn't be too difficult," said Carol acidly.

"Yes, I'm seeing him again tonight," said Maggie Dimond. She spared Carol an amused glance. "It's no particular hardship."

"You really want to go ahead with all of this, Maggie?" asked Gaunt. "You're quite sure?"

"Yes."

He sighed. "Why?"

"Why not?" she countered. "I'm old enough to know what I'm doing, even if it is just for the hell of it."

"All right." Gaunt gave up. "But one other thing. When Stepan goes on his 'survey trip' tonight, I go too. I want to see the set-up for myself."

Valachova shrugged.

"Come about ten tonight," he suggested. "And bring a waterproof —the weather forecast is this rain will get worse."

They left Valachova and Maggie Dimond a few minutes later. Carol got into the passenger seat of the Skoda in stony silence and stayed that way as Gaunt set the little coupe moving, its windscreen wipers slapping against the drizzle.

It was several minutes before she spoke. By then, they were on their way along the network of country roads towards the main through route for Prague.

"You're a damned fool," she said suddenly. "You're letting them use you."

"It works both ways." Gaunt kept his eyes on the narrow twisting road. "Whatever I do, it won't be for Maggie Dimond or Valachova, or anybody's jewels, believe me."

"I know that." She bit her lip. "But Garr isn't on his own. What can you do?"

"There'll be a way." He made it sound confident, a lot more confident than he felt. "And you stay out of it." He gave a quick, sideways glance that stopped her half-formed protest. "Listen, so far Matthew Garr doesn't know about you. At most, you're just someone I've taken out a couple of times. Let's keep him thinking that way."

"I'm available and female?" She scowled. "Thanks." Then she gave a half-smile and nodded. "I suppose it makes sense. If—"

"If I've got you in reserve, it's going to help," Gaunt assured her. He eased back on the accelerator and took the Skoda past a plodding horse and cart, almost brushing the cart's side in the process. The farmer perched on the cart gave them a cheerful nod.

"What have you got planned for the rest of the day?"

"Now?" She glanced at her wrist-watch. "Well, there are some Czech electronics people who expect me to show up at their plant. There's a formal dinner tonight, for accredited foreign representatives. But—"

"Stick with that programme," he suggested, accelerating again. "I'll contact you, one way or another, if anything starts happening."

She hesitated. "If that's a promise."

"Cross my heart." He gave her a wink.

"All right," she said resignedly. "Where will you be?"

"This afternoon?" He rubbed a hand along his chin, feeling the bristles, remembering he hadn't shaved that morning. "Once I'm cleaned up, I'll maybe spend an afternoon at the Trade Fair. Let myself get caught up in the romance of industry. Or have a snooze in a corner."

"Go to hell," she said with mock indignation. Then her voice changed and she added quietly, "Be careful. Please."

Once back in Prague, he dropped Carol in a shopping street a short taxi ride from the Smetana Hotel. For the time being, he felt it was better they weren't seen together. From there, he drove to the hotel, parked the Skoda in the square across from the main entrance, then went into the hotel and up to his room.

He still had the Luger. He left it on the dressing table while he washed, shaved, and put on a clean shirt. Dressed again, he frowned at the pistol then decided that at the very least he should keep it available.

It was back in the waistband of his trousers when he left the hotel again and got into the Skoda. But once aboard he jammed the weapon under the front passenger seat, where it would be easy to reach.

No one followed him when he drove away. He spent several minutes making sure of that, checking his rear-view mirror, doubling in his own tracks. At last satisfied, he made a right turn at the next junction and took the road for the exhibition centre.

It was after 1 P.M. when he got there and parked the Skoda. He had a sandwich and a glass of beer in the Trade Fair cafeteria, then he stayed on, making a slow business of smoking a cigarette.

At last, reluctantly, he decided it was time to move on. If anyone was watching, it had to appear as if Jonathan Gaunt was making a close, professional study of all the Trade Fair had to offer.

After the first couple of hours it amounted to a recipe for total boredom. Working his way down one exhibition lane then back up the next, collecting sales leaflets here and there, occasionally talking to some enthusiastic stand representative, smiling cheerfully when he said goodbye, Gaunt reached the stage of loathing everything in sight.

His mind was busy in a totally different direction, trying to plan, to assemble possibilities, to make some kind of sensible pattern out of what lay ahead.

It didn't happen. His feet were sore and his back began its familiar low-key ache. He returned to the cafeteria, dumped the leaflets in the men's room, then ordered a cup of coffee. Half-way through drinking it, a hand slapped his shoulder and he looked up, startled.

"Found you—good." It was John Alford. The plump, red-faced glass buyer had his wife in tow, as usual. She stood a few paces back, giving Gaunt a weak smile. Alford's breath was heavy with alcohol as he leaned over the table. "Some people have been looking for you, Gaunt."

"Here?" Gaunt looked at him blankly.

"No." Alford scratched his small moustache and gave what was meant to be a friendly grin. "Back at the hotel—a couple of plain-clothes police. Something about a statement you're to give them."

"That's right." Gaunt nodded, hiding his relief. "What else did they say?"

"That was it. I just thought you'd better know." Alford grimaced. "Police! Around here they're more like gorillas in disguise. Take last night—"

"I heard you had a problem," murmured Gaunt politely.

"Right." Alford nodded vigorously. "But I don't take that kind of treatment. Told them to get the hell out of it, or say goodbye to every damned order I've placed." He winked. "That fixed them. Off they went, trailing their knuckles. Uh—" he leaned closer. For a moment his small eyes considered Gaunt with a surprising shrewdness. "You all right? I mean—no real problems? If there are—"

"It's just a statement." Quickly Gaunt shook his head. "But thanks for the offer."

"You need me, you call me. Or that wife of mine, if I'm not around." Alford stood back and beamed. "We Brits have to stick together, eh?"

He ambled off to join his wife. Glad to be rid of him, Gaunt abandoned the rest of his coffee and left the cafeteria.

At least Alford, without knowing it, had given him one clear warning. Going back to the hotel might mean finding the two policemen still waiting. Even if it was only for that promised statement, it was the kind of interview which might lead to complications—and complications he could do without.

Valachova had said to come back at ten that night. It meant he had still several hours to kill. But there was one thing he wanted to do, had to do in that time.

The drizzle of rain had ended when Gaunt finally left the exhibition hall. There were still dark clouds overhead and the forecast of heavier rain might still come true. The roads were dry again as he got back aboard the Skoda and set it moving.

He reached the centre of Prague in time to meet the start of the evening rush-hour traffic. Whatever other forms of discipline the

Czechs had to accept, their driving had a fierce independent edge. It showed, whether they were in control of a lumbering tram or straddling one of the scores of light-weight motor cycles erupting from unsuspected parking lots.

Gaunt fought his way through the noisy tangle of traffic and headed south-east, back to the shabby, narrow street where Janos Barta had lived and died.

Dusk was closing in. The first street lamps were coming to life and curtains were being closed at some of the windows above him. The entrance door to Janos Barta's block lay open. There was no one in sight. Gaunt parked outside it, got out, and climbed the worn stairs to Barta's door.

There was no doorbell. He knocked, waited, then knocked again. At last it opened and a young girl looked out. He recognized her as the girl who'd kept watch at street level when he'd visited that morning. She looked surprised, then gave him a polite nod.

"Everyone has gone, Mr. Gaunt," she said in slow, careful English. "All is—yes, completed here."

"And his sister?" asked Gaunt.

"Gone too," said the girl. "She has relatives, in the country." She gave him a slight smile. "I stayed to—well, tidy. You understand?"

He nodded, then stopped her as she made to close the door.

"Does she need anything?"

"His sister?" The girl shook her head. "Only what she has lost, Mr. Gaunt. But she does not blame you. None of us does."

The door closed. He stood for a moment, sighed, then went back down to the car.

It became dark, still without the threatened rain. Gaunt drove out of the area, stopped at a bar, located its pay phone, and dialled the Hotel Smetana. There was no reply when the hotel switchboard tried Carol Marek's room. He shrugged and smiled to himself as he replaced the receiver. Carol, at least, was out of things for the moment. If possible, for her sake, he intended to keep it that way.

For a while, he nursed a brandy in the bar. But the atmosphere around was unfriendly, the tables nearest his own stayed empty. He was a stranger. Strangers could mean a police informer, trouble in some form.

He left. There was a cinema further down the street, a concrete box of a place with peeling paintwork and a damp, stale smell. He paid for a ticket and went in, settling in one of the hard-backed seats. The main feature film was about a peasant girl who came to town and found love and purpose in a factory *brigada*. Only the back rows of the cinema were full and the customers there had little interest in the screen.

The night was still dry when he left, though with a cold wind. He got back into the Skoda and set it moving again.

The drive to his meeting with Stepan Valachova took half an hour. It was just after 10 P.M. when the car's tyres crunched over the loose gravel of the driveway which led up to the old castle. Gaunt stopped in a shadowed area of the parking lot and got out. At first glance, the whole building was in darkness. Then he saw a small light burning above a side-door. He went over, knocked on the door, and after a moment it swung open. Stepan Valachova came out, nodded a greeting, and closed the door behind him.

"You decided to come." Valachova gave an approving grunt, his bearded face a silhouette in the night. He was wearing a long, dark coat and a knitted cap and had a small haversack slung over one shoulder. He considered Gaunt for a moment. "I want one thing agreed, Mr. Gaunt. I am in charge in this small adventure, whatever happens."

"You're in charge," agreed Gaunt.

"Good." Valachova smiled approvingly. "We will use your car— we might as well travel in comfort."

They got into the Skoda, Valachova in the passenger seat and nursing the haversack on his lap. Then, Gaunt following the man's directions, they set off.

It was a twenty-minute journey, along more country roads. Gaunt saw an occasional farmhouse or cottage, but they were usually in darkness. The only other traffic they encountered was a solitary tractor which came lumbering towards them out of the night. Relaxed back in the passenger seat, Valachova hummed under his breath most of the way. But his humming stopped as a glow appeared ahead.

"Slow down," he instructed. "Not too much—then drive normally, carefully. Don't stop."

Gaunt obeyed. A moment later they rounded a bend in the road. The glow became a pool of light further down the road and they began travelling beside a high fence which had concrete posts and was topped with barbed wire. He could see huts and the vague shapes of lines of trucks and other vehicles.

"Keep going," murmured Valachova. "But look and remember."

The road broadened at the pool of light, the floodlit main gate to the camp. It had a guard-post and a Russian soldier, the collar of his greatcoat turned up, huddled in the shelter of a small sentry-box beside a barrier pole.

They passed through the pool of light and left the gate behind, the fence still continuing.

"On your right, Mr. Gaunt," said Valachova.

Gaunt nodded. The Skoda's headlamps had already picked up the grey-white stone of a small religious shrine on the opposite side of the road from the camp. Set a few feet back from the verge, it had a sad, neglected air. Weeds and scrub had grown around it. Someone had spray-painted a slogan across the front, where the inner niche was an empty eye staring at the barbed wire opposite.

"That's it?"

"Yes." Valachova nodded. "In about half a kilometre there's a small road on your right. Take it."

The road came up. It was little more than a track and the Skoda bumped and bounced over the pot-holed surface. Then Valachova grunted and signalled Gaunt to pull in. They stopped under the shelter of some trees.

Switching off engine and lights, Gaunt followed Valachova out of the car. The ground underfoot was hard with frost and the wind was cold enough to make him fasten the buttons of his sheepskin.

"Do you have your pistol?" asked Valachova.

"Yes." Gaunt showed him the Luger, which he'd collected from its hiding place.

"Put it away," said Valachova. He slung the haversack over his shoulder again as he spoke. "We won't need it. Not tonight. Now—stay close, do as I do."

They set off through the trees. On the far side, at the start of a field, the glow of light which marked the camp-gate was again visible in the distance. Pointing towards it, Valachova began walking. A dark shape loomed ahead, became a low dry-stone wall, and they scrambled over it into another field. The ground there had been ploughed and walking was more difficult but Valachova didn't slow his pace.

Eventually, about half-way across, he stopped.

"From now on, go carefully," he instructed in a low voice.

"I had that notion already," said Gaunt dryly.

He cursed under his breath as they set off again, trudging over the furrows, the ground alternately rising then dipping, the night darkness concealing the constant likelihood of a pitfall that could break an ankle.

The glow of light became very near as they trudged up still another low rise. Valachova signalled him down and they crawled the rest of the way, then lay side by side at the top, looking down at the rear of the wayside shrine. It was no more than a stone's throw away at the foot of a short, gentle, unploughed slope. To their left and across the road, the main gate of the army camp was near enough for them to see the lone Russian soldier still huddled in his sentry-box.

"This will do." Easing on his side, Valachova produced a pair of binoculars from his haversack. He used them for a moment, focussing on the sentry, then gave a pleased murmur. "Yes, I know him. Next time I remember to go to church I must give thanks for the Russian system—they are creatures of habit."

"So?" Gaunt shifted his position slightly, puzzled. "How about explaining what we're doing?"

"Checking, Mr. Gaunt," soothed Valachova. "Making sure." He used the binoculars again, but for longer, scanning the area from the gate to the shrine. Then he passed them over. "Take a look."

Gaunt had to adjust the focus first. Valachova was apparently short-sighted in one eye. Taking his time, Gaunt began at the shrine. The powerful lenses brought the stonework up close. Beside it, the scrub beside the road verge formed a flimsy screen which, by night, would probably give adequate shelter for anyone working down there—provided they kept low and stayed quiet.

From there to the sentry-post at the camp-gate, he estimated, wasn't much more than half the length of a football field. He watched the sentry for a moment, seeing the man's boredom, catching a half-stifled yawn. Grinning in sympathy, he lowered the glasses.

"The spot where we'll dig is about two metres back from the shrine," murmured Valachova. "I calculate we'll have to go down about a metre."

He scowled at Valachova. "What makes you so sure?"

Valachova grinned, his teeth showing white in the darkness.

"Well?" asked Gaunt.

"I told you I was better equipped this time," reminded Valachova dryly. "We had to dig and dig before we found the silver. Here"—he shook his head—"these Russians make that impossible. But the last chest was made of metal. So I read some books. I made myself a metal-detector—"

"You used it down there?" Gaunt stared at the bearded man in near disbelief. "If you'd been caught—"

"It was at night. I was careful," said Valachova, unperturbed. "The detector gave a clear reading, at just one place."

Gaunt sighed, rested his head on his arms, and looked across the darkness of the field to the floodlit gate and guard-post.

"What about them?" he demanded. "Suppose you're digging, suppose you hit a stone with the spade? Any kind of noise and the sentry could turn out the rest of the guard, have them down on top of you."

"That's the main reason I came tonight, Mr. Gaunt," said Valachova patiently. "I have studied this camp, by day and by night. The Russians use it only as a storage depot, a reserve base for military transport. The unit manning it is less than company strength—and they work a regular weekly rota when it comes to the night guard on that gate."

Something small, fast, and unseen scurried along one of the nearby furrows. They heard it, then a moment later something else in the night gave a quick, high death squeal. Gaunt winced and glanced at Valachova again.

"What's important about the rota?"

"The rota and tomorrow night," corrected Valachova simply. "It's the night of the week when the guard is commanded by a certain corporal." He smiled a little. "The corporal seems to have a woman friend in the next village. At least, he disappears from the camp for several hours. When he goes, the sentry at the gate waits a little while then joins his friends in the guard-hut."

"If you know so much, why haven't you tried digging before?" asked Gaunt.

Valachova shrugged. "Finding out took time. Then—well, I am not a fool. While I dig, I need someone keeping watch. For that, until now, there was only Mrs. Dimond—and she insists it is her right."

"Which makes you both crazy," Gaunt told him. He shifted where he lay, shivering again. "And this ground's rock-hard."

"Only the top skin," said Valachova. He eased back as he spoke, then rose to a low crouch. "At this time of year the frost goes no deeper. Two hours, Mr. Gaunt—that's all at most and it is finished. If some soldier finds a hole the next morning, who cares?"

They made their way back across the fields to the car. As soon as they were aboard, Gaunt set the heater going. The engine had cooled but the blast of lukewarm air around his feet still amounted to luxury. He turned to Valachova and made one last try.

"Ever thought of what will happen if you're caught?"

"Yes," admitted Valachova. "But I prefer to think positive, Mr. Gaunt—to consider what will happen if I'm not."

Gaunt gave up. He tucked the Luger back in its hiding place under the front seat, started the car, and set it moving.

The time was close on midnight when he dropped Valachova off at the castle. The man thanked him with a nod and didn't look back as he walked away. Gaunt turned the Skoda in the parking lot, fumbled for his cigarettes and lit one as he drove back down the driveway.

As he reached the road, it began to rain—slight at first, then a steady downpour. He switched on the wipers and scowled as they slapped busily. Rain would soften the ground, make Valachova's task easier. Sighing, Gaunt caught himself wishing for a moment that the man would dig himself a hole, fall in it, and drown in the stuff.

Valachova's plan was a wild, uncomplicated gamble. So wild and uncomplicated it might succeed. Even if it did, even if Valachova succeeded in sneaking his buried treasure out from under the noses of the Russian guards, it wasn't by any means finished.

There was Colonel Brozman—and there was Matthew Garr. Whistling tunelessly to himself, Gaunt kept the Skoda moving as its headlamp beams lanced into the rain and darkness.

The Czech security colonel remained an unknown factor in the background. But Matthew Garr would be waiting, ready to move and ready to regard killing as an incidental.

Unless someone stopped him first.

The rain eased off after a spell. It was a little more than a drizzle when he began driving through the outskirts of Prague, amost stopped when he drew in and parked in the square opposite the Smetana Hotel.

Gaunt was out of the car when he remembered the Luger. Opening the driver's door again, he reached across and felt under the front passenger seat. Then he swore slowly and pungently. The pistol had gone. Valachova must have taken it during the drive back to the castle.

There was nothing he could do about it. Locking the car, he walked across the square and into the hotel. There were no messages for him at reception and even allowing for the hour the lobby looked unusually quiet.

"The Trade Fair dinner," explained the desk clerk in the bored voice of a man who was on duty until 7 A.M. whatever happened. "Government functions always start late and finish later." He paused, then with a shade more interest, added, "If you're looking for company—"

Gaunt shook his head. He'd already noted the cluster of girls waiting petulantly in the lobby bar, their business having a bad night.

He went up to his room. If Carol had been back he'd have gone to her, talked to her, told her what had happened that evening.

But she was still out there somewhere, getting the full official welcome treatment. He yawned, shrugged, and got ready for bed.

They came for him at 3 A.M. Gaunt was asleep when his room door was opened. He wakened with the light being switched on, then someone was shaking his shoulder.

There were two of them, broad-built men with belted raincoats, close-cut hair, and totally expressionless faces. Another of the same pattern was standing at the opened door.

"Police," said the man who had shaken him awake. He had eyes like ice-water and his voice held complete disinterest. One hand flicked a black-bound warrant card under Gaunt's nose. "You are to come with us."

They checked his clothes before they allowed him to dress. Then he was escorted along to the elevator and down to the lobby.

It was deserted. One of his escorts took a deceptively light finger-and-thumb grip of Gaunt's jacket sleeve and he was hustled out into the night and straight into a waiting car. As soon as the three men were aboard, it pulled away.

"Where are you taking me?" asked Gaunt.

He wasn't answered. The car purred on through the empty streets then swung into a square which fronted an impressively large building with a high, colonnaded front. It was partly floodlit, had its own flag-poles, and the uniformed sentries at the foot of its broad flight of steps weren't police.

The car murmured past a sign on the edge of a parking area. Its headlamps caught the wording, repeated in four languages, "Entry Permitted Only to Vehicles of the Federal Ministry of Foreign Affairs."

Gaunt sighed. "Colonel Brozman?"

The man on his left gave a slight grin and a fractional nod.

The car stopped at a side-entrance. He was taken out, then led across to the entrance where another uniformed guard was waiting. Inside, his jacket sleeve still in the same grip, Gaunt was hustled along a brightly lit corridor which had a dark-red composition floor and white-tiled walls.

They stopped him at a door, opened it, and thumbed him in. The door slammed shut behind him. He was in a small, windowless room with the same composition floor and tiled walls. There was a table and chair, both bolted to the floor. An extractor fan hummed high on one wall and the room light was set in a metal fixture in the ceiling.

In all his life, Jonathan Gaunt had never felt quite so much on his own.

CHAPTER 8

There was a spyhole on the door. Every now and again Jonathan Gaunt had a feeling someone was using it for a moment, checking on him. Very occasionally he heard footsteps. Once there was a shout, another time he heard laughter.

But that was all. Time crept past as if he'd been forgotten. They had left him his wrist-watch and anything that had been in his pockets, and he smoked a cigarette. That left five in the pack. Grimly he decided it might be a good idea to keep them for later.

Four hours passed. Then, a little after 7 A.M., a key turned in a lock and the door swung open. Two of the men who'd brought him from the Smetana stood in the doorway and one beckoned. Shrugging, Gaunt went out with them into the corridor. They led him to a wash-room. One handed him soap, a clean towel, and a small, battery-powered electric razor.

He didn't need any further invitation. His two guards leaned against the wall, talking idly, while he washed and shaved. He felt better by the time he'd finished and they beckoned again.

He was led further along the same corridor, then up a short flight of stairs into another corridor where there was a carpet on the floor. One of the men tapped on an oak-panelled door. A voice barked a muffled reply and the guard opened the door, thumbing Gaunt through.

Gaunt went in. The door closed softly behind him.

"Good morning," said a dry, laconic voice. Colonel Anatole Brozman sat behind a large, leather-topped desk in the middle of the room, framed in the bright sunlight pouring in through a broad window behind him. The Czech security man was immaculate in a dark business suit, white shirt, and black tie and he nodded towards a chair placed in front of his desk. "Sit down, please, Mr. Gaunt."

"Thank you." Stonily Gaunt crossed over to the chair, sat down, and glanced around. Brozman's office was plainly furnished but everything was of the best. Probably the only thing that had come out of Foreign Office stock was the large map of Czechoslovakia covering most of one wall. An unexpected touch was a bowl of spring daffodils, a yellow splash of colour on a table by the window. He looked at Brozman. "Nice morning—what I can see of it."

"It is." Brozman gave a short chuckle, showing his teeth for a moment. "No indignation, Mr. Gaunt? No demand to see your Embassy people?"

"Maybe later." Gaunt stretched and yawned with a controlled deliberation. "Isn't this when you're supposed to say someone made a mistake?"

"It could be." Brozman leaned back, clasping his hands behind his close-clipped grey hair. "I could suggest that certain—ah—instructions I gave were interpreted too literally." His mouth hardened. "On the other hand, perhaps I wanted to teach you a lesson—one with minimal discomfort but its own warning."

"Why?" asked Gaunt.

"For some good reasons." Brozman eyed him with slow deliberation. "I'll give you one as a start. The body of a man was found among some bushes at Prague Castle late yesterday afternoon. He had no identification, he had died of a broken neck, and he was wearing a shoulder harness for a pistol—though there was no sign of the weapon."

"Maybe he left it at home," murmured Gaunt.

"Perhaps. But we did find a knife." Brozman brought his hands from behind his head and leaned forward. "A medical examiner places time of death at about twenty-four hours earlier. One of the castle guides has told us of a man she saw create a disturbance the previous day, then run off, pursued by another stranger."

Gaunt nodded helpfully. "You asked me about that."

"She has seen the dead man and has identified him as the second stranger," snapped Brozman impatiently. "That leaves the mystery of the man he was chasing. You were at the castle around that time."

"So were a lot of other people," murmured Gaunt defensively.

"Yes." Brozman's eyes glinted angrily. "But you still claim you know nothing about it?"

"Nothing." Gaunt shook his head. "Why don't you ask your witness about me?"

"We did," said Brozman. "Earlier this morning. She took a look at you downstairs, through the observation hole. Unfortunately, she can't be sure."

"Then that's that, isn't it?" parried Gaunt.

"No." Brozman slammed a fist on his leather desk-top. "Don't strain my patience, Mr. Gaunt. I want to know why you're here, why you came to Prague."

"The Trade Fair."

"That?" Brozman sneered at the thought. "It makes a good story —and, yes, I agree you are a civil servant. I've checked. You also work for some obscure department with no particular history of being involved in espionage as such. But the rest of your story?" Brozman shook his head. "I don't believe it."

"That's my hard luck," said Gaunt. "What am I supposed to do about it?"

"See sense," urged Brozman. "Let me remind you of something, Mr. Gaunt. You came here on a tourist visa, you don't hold a diplomatic passport—"

"So I can't claim diplomatic immunity," agreed Gaunt. He paused, assessing his chances, finding them very low, then suggested, "But I could still be trouble, Colonel. Try holding me, and there are people who wouldn't like it."

"I'm aware of that. There is also another situation which—" Brozman stopped short and swore under his breath, as if angered by his own indiscretion. For a long moment he frowned down at his desk. Then, at last, he looked up. "I happen to have my own priorities in this matter. They may not be exactly what you would expect."

"Try me," invited Gaunt.

"Perhaps I will," said Brozman. He got up and moved heavily to stand with his back to the door so that Gaunt had to half-turn in his chair to keep him in view. "Later today I am going to a funeral, Mr. Gaunt. The funeral of the man who was murdered in the street the night you arrived." He pursed his lips. "You tried to help him. That's the main reason why, in a little while, I'm going to let you walk out of this building."

"You said you didn't know him," said Gaunt.

"I lied," said Brozman flatly. "I work in an area where lies come easily when necessary. His name was Josef Kosek, he was a captain in our security services, and he was also a friend." He paused. "A close friend—and in this profession, such friends are rare. Now, more than anything else at this moment, I want the men who killed him."

The temptation was there, and it took an effort to resist it. Gaunt shook his head.

"I can't help you, Colonel."

"No?" Brozman came over and looked down at him. "Even Captain Kosek didn't know why he was attacked or who the men were. He managed to tell the police that much before he died." He shrugged. "All he was doing that night was a more or less normal surveillance duty. I see no possibility of a connection."

"Then maybe he was just unlucky, walked into something else," suggested Gaunt.

"Yes." Brozman stepped back. "But think about it. This once, I might be prepared to ignore some aspects which might embarrass— if it got me what I want." He stopped there, gave a grimace, and his manner changed as he glanced at his watch. "Have you had breakfast?"

Gaunt shook his head.

"I still want a formal statement about what happened that night. Someone will take it. Then, by the time you've eaten, it should be ready for signing." Brozman went over to his desk and pressed a bell-push. "Later, of course, if you decide you remember anything more—" He left it there as the door opened.

The two men who came in were his escorts from earlier. Brozman spoke to them briefly. They nodded. One came over and tapped Gaunt on the shoulder.

Brozman signalled them to wait. "Mr. Gaunt, I'm curious about one thing. The advice I had about you said you were once an army officer but were invalided out. I saw the tie you wore last night. You were a paratrooper?"

Gaunt nodded.

"I thought so." Brozman gave a humourless grin. "That would include unarmed combat training. Yes, you could break someone's neck quite easily—even if he had a knife."

He gave a gesture of dismissal and Gaunt was taken away.

It took another hour. First, he had to give his formal statement to a shirt-sleeved official who wrote everything in laborious longhand. They brought him a mug of coffee and a fried-egg sandwich, and he had to wait while the same official pecked two-fingered style at a typewriter. At last, the result was placed in front of him, and he signed it.

Afterwards, he was led along another corridor and turned loose outside the building. The sun was still shining and felt particularly warm and friendly. The parking lot was beginning to fill with cars. Office workers were arriving for the start of their day, greeting each other, gossiping.

Gaunt drew a deep, thankful breath of the city air, paused long enough to light one of his carefully hoarded cigarettes, then walked out past the two armed, fur-capped sentries.

The main street was busy with traffic, the pavements crowded. Prague's morning rush-hour was under way. He kept walking without particularly caring where he was heading.

He knew he'd been lucky, that by comparison with what could have happened he'd received almost kid-glove treatment, but he was under no illusion that Anatole Brozman had finished with him.

Yet maybe there was a possibility in it all. Maybe, with a little more luck, there might be some kind of a trade he could offer Brozman—a trade that could work.

There were traffic lights ahead. He had to stop in a jam of pedestrians, all waiting for the lights to change, and at the same time recognized a department store across the street. He was only a few minutes' walk from what suddenly seemed home, his hotel room.

Something hard jabbed into his left side. Simultaneously a hand gripped his right arm.

"Just act friendly, Mr. Gaunt," murmured a voice in his ear.

He froze. On his left he was flanked by the man in the brown suit who'd been with Matthew Garr the previous day. The man on his right was a stranger, young, slightly built, with a thin, vicious face.

"You know what this is," said the man on his left, softly. He had a coat draped over his right arm. The muzzle of the concealed gun in his hand jabbed again into Gaunt's side as the traffic lights changed. "Walk."

They crossed the street and kept walking. A car drew in at the pavement's edge, an old white Mercedes. When they reached it, Gaunt was bundled into the rear seat with one of his captors on either side.

"What do you want?" asked Gaunt.

The man in the brown suit hefted the gun in his hand and shrugged. He nodded to their driver and the car began moving.

They travelled north with the traffic, crossed one of the bridges over the river. A few kilometres on, they reached an industrial area. Going down a lane at the side of a factory building, the Mercedes drove into what appeared to be a small, disused builder's yard and stopped. Roughly bundled out, Gaunt was taken towards a dilapidated two-storey building then in through a door. He could hear the car driving away as he was pushed up a flight of creaking wooden stairs and shoved into a shabbily furnished room.

"Against the wall," he was ordered. "Face it."

A fist slammed cruelly against the small of his back to hurry him on. Hands against the peeling wallpaper, he winced as his legs were casually kicked apart. One of the men made a quick, patting search of his clothes then his arms were jerked down behind his back and his wrists were tightly tied with thin, strong cord.

"Turn."

He obeyed. The man in the brown suit gave a sneering grin and cuffed him casually across the mouth. Gaunt felt the taste of blood on his lips and heard the second man chuckle.

"Where's your boss?" he asked. He remembered the names Janos Barta had given him. "You're Leiber and Zelagny, right? the errand boys. Maybe you'd better wait till he gets here."

The men exchanged a surprised glance. Frowning, the younger man came over. Pushing Gaunt on the chest, he tripped him. Helpless, Gaunt fell backwards and went down on the floor. One of them kicked him. Then they turned away, brought two chairs over to a table, and sat there.

About an hour passed. One of the men got up, went through to a small kitchen, and made coffee. He brought back two mugs and gave Gaunt another casual kick in the ribs as he went back to the table.

Twice Gaunt tried to get them to speak. His attempts were ignored, and he gave up. A brief experiment told him that the cord tying his wrists was too tight and too well knotted to yield to anything he could hope to do.

He was in trouble, worse trouble than he'd been in Colonel Brozman's hands. But the way Garr's men had snatched him in the street, in daylight, did tell him one thing, that Matthew Garr had his own problems. Garr was being forced to take any risk necessary.

The thought didn't help in terms of his own immediate future.

At last, he heard a car draw up outside. The engine note told him it was the Mercedes. His two captors rose quickly, went over to a window, looked out, and relaxed. One hurried out of the room and downstairs. Gaunt heard the door at the bottom open, a murmur of voices, then footsteps coming up.

"Sorry to keep you waiting, Mr. Gaunt," said a sarcastic, slightly high-pitched voice. "I expected those STB people would turn you loose eventually—they work that way. But I couldn't be sure when."

Gaunt looked round as Matthew Garr walked over and stopped beside him. Garr was neatly dressed as usual, his black fur hat shoved back on his broad, balding head. The man gave an amused smile which twisted as it met the scar on his cheek.

"We don't need to be introduced, do we?" he asked.

"No." Gaunt met the smile calmly. "And I got a lot friendlier handling in the last place."

Garr shrugged. "Things could get worse for you."

"The way they were for Janos Barta?" asked Gaunt bitterly.

"Barta—yes, he said that was his name." Garr pursed his lips. "It could have been easier for him if he hadn't tried to be stubborn. Still, now we have you." He signalled to the man waiting in the background. They dragged Gaunt along the floor and left him in a sitting position with his back against the nearest wall. Garr followed them over. "Now we can talk, eh?"

"About Barta?"

Matthew Garr sighed and glanced at the man nearest him. "Leiber—"

The man in the brown suit stepped forward. Gaunt took another cuff across the mouth, hard enough to knock his head back.

"About the Dimond woman, and your interest," said Garr, his high-pitched voice reaching an almost piping note. "Beginning back at her home in Scotland, Mr. Gaunt. I wondered about the 'police-man' who turned up there at the wrong moment. It was you, I presume?"

Gaunt nodded.

"That's the worst of local hired help." Garr shook his head in disgust. "They were in too much of a rush to get away to care about anything else. Still—then you follow Mrs. Dimond out here. You claim to be some kind of civil servant, and—knowing the Czechs—they would verify that for themselves." He paused and rubbed his chin. "But of course your real reason for being involved, for being such an annoyance, is something else. Tell me about it."

"Or?" asked Gaunt.

Garr sighed. "Or you get a bullet through one kneecap, then the other. I have an Irish friend who says it is remarkably painful—he now lives in a wheelchair."

More than anything, Garr's calm, matter-of-fact manner showed he meant it. Half a truth would be better than an attempt at lying, but Gaunt knew he had to have the timing right.

"Suppose I tell you?" he asked suspiciously. "What about afterwards?"

"Afterwards . . . I'm not sure. You've caused me trouble, Gaunt. The man you killed, Radiki, was probably my best—which tells me something about you." He shrugged. "Fortunately, I had more help available. But—no, I'm not sure yet. It may depend on you."

Gaunt scowled at him. "I need a better deal than that."

"Do you?" mused Garr. He turned his head. "Leiber, the right knee I think."

Leiber nodded, and stepped forward. The gun in his hand, a snub-nosed revolver, was a .38 of uncertain make.

"All right." Gaunt didn't have to try too hard to get sufficient urgency into his voice. "Don't be so damned hasty." He waited while Garr gestured the man back, then moistened his lips. "I'm on loan to the British Inland Revenue to investigate Maggie Dimond."

"Why?"

"They were worried. She was spending too much money." He added what he hoped would be a useful embroidery. "A lot of it in Swiss francs. Tax persons who get involved in crooked sidelines aren't popular."

"I see." Garr rubbed his chin, his eyes hard, obviously thinking. "What else?"

"We discovered you were involved."

"And I've got a certain reputation?" Garr shaped a slight, understanding smile, which had no warmth. "Then you followed her to

Prague. Why warn her at the castle?" He snapped finger and thumb together and answered his own question. "You recognized me that first night—"

"When your team murdered one of Colonel Brozman's people and tried to grab Maggie's friend," agreed Gaunt wearily.

"Yes." Garr's manner suddenly hardened again. "What do you know about her friend?"

"The bearded man?" Gaunt shook his head. "Not much. His first name is Stepan. I tried to get more out of her, but she told me to go to hell."

"That part I can believe," said Garr. His high-pitched voice softened persuasively. "You're doing fine, being sensible. Now tell me this—and I want the truth. How much else do you know, Mr. Gaunt?"

"About what's going on?" Gaunt looked steadily at the man's broad, scarred face. "That it's something big, probably a deal that's gone sour. Drugs maybe—I don't know. But it looks like you can't sort it out until you've got Maggie Dimond and her pal."

"I wonder—" Garr drew a slow, deep breath. He turned on his heel, walked over to the window, and looked out for a moment. Then he came back. "You were taken from your hotel at 3 A.M.— I got word of that. The STB people had you for several hours. How much of all this did they ask you, how much did you tell them?"

"They're only interested in the security man who was killed," said Gaunt. He gave what he hoped was a convincing sigh. "You picked a beauty. He was one of their middle management—a captain. They still have the idea I could tell them more. But if I did—"

"You'd find it awkward." Garr gave a cross between a laugh and a giggle. He leaned forward. Suddenly his clenched fist swung a chopping blow which took Gaunt hard on the side of the head, making him grunt with pain. "Where do we find this man Stepan?"

"I don't know." Gaunt didn't have to fake his dazed response. "I've tried, yes. But I don't know."

"Maybe you're telling the truth. If you're lying"—Garr's face came down close to his own—"we'll find out. There won't be a second chance for you."

Gaunt nodded. His head hurt.

Leaving him, Matthew Garr beckoned the other two men and they followed him into another room. Gaunt heard a murmur of voices, with Garr apparently doing most of the talking. Then they came back.

"I've things to do," said Garr. "Leiber will keep an eye on you. But first we'll make you a little more—no, not comfortable, but secure."

Jerked to his feet, Gaunt was taken through to the other room. It held an old, iron-framed bed with an ancient mattress. Pushed down on it, covered by Leiber's revolver, he had to submit while his ankles were tied together then lashed to one of the iron rails at the bottom of the bed. Leiber took another length of cord and fashioned a slip-knot loop at one end.

The loop went round Gaunt's neck. The other end, with a small amount of slack, was tied to one of the top bedrails.

"To make sure you behave," said Garr smoothly. "Try anything foolish and—" He put his hand up to his neck and made a mock choking noise.

They left him. Soon he heard the car outside start up and draw away. A little later, Leiber came into the room, looked down at him, and gave the cord behind Gaunt's head an experimental tug. Gaunt felt the cord bite into his neck, brought his head back to ease the strain, and Leiber tightened it again.

Beginning to choke, Gaunt fought for breath. Then, grinning, Leiber released his grip, turned on his heel, and walked out.

Gaunt slumped against the lumpy mattress. It had a stale, damp odour and one section near his head looked as though it had been nibbled by mice or something larger. The room had a single, grimy window and the only other furniture was a rickety chest of drawers. When he moved his head, the cord immediately made itself felt.

He was helpless. Carefully he eased himself into as comfortable a position as possible. For the moment, about all he could do was concentrate on keeping things that way.

Whatever was happening outside, there was nothing he could do about it. He grimaced at the dingy ceiling. Maggie Dimond and Valachova were on their own again without knowing it, but his real worry was Carol. She'd wait, for a little while at least. After that, she might try anything.

That could be bad for Carol. It could be even worse for him.

Time passed. He heard Leiber moving about and the man looked in a few times but didn't repeat his experiment with the noose.

Gaunt settled into a steady routine of slight, positive movements to try to fight off the worst of the cramp in his limbs. He tried to measure the hours from the way the shadows thrown by the sunlight coming through the grimy window gradually moved around the room.

He made it late afternoon when he heard the car return and stop in the yard below. After a minute or two he heard voices in the other room. Then Garr came in. He looked pleased with himself as he sat on the edge of the bed.

"So far, you may have been telling the truth," he declared with a dry satisfaction. "That's good. Want anything?" He chuckled as he saw Gaunt's expression. "Anything reasonable, I mean."

Gaunt nodded. "A drink. Plain ordinary water." His throat felt parched.

"All right." Garr lit a cigarette and carefully blew the smoke towards the ceiling. "Leiber says you're behaving. That's sensible."

"Thanks," said Gaunt sarcastically. "What's going on Garr? What are you trying to pull now?"

Garr shrugged. "Mostly, I'm waiting. From what I can gather, one or two people are worried about what's happened to you. They've been assured you were released by the security police, but that's not good enough for them."

"You've a good ear to the ground," said Gaunt. "How much does he cost?"

"Quite a lot. He's one of the reception staff." Garr pursed his lips. "Then, of course, you've cost me some additional, unexpected expense. I had to find this place and another car—and an extra man." He got to his feet. "Tell me something. Why would Mrs. Dimond go out this morning and buy a pair of heavy walking shoes?"

Gaunt shook his head.

"It doesn't matter. I think I know." Garr's scarred face twitched a fractional smile. "Yes. With a little luck, this should soon be over. For all of us, Mr. Gaunt."

He went out. A few minutes later, the car drove away.

It was another quarter hour before Leiber came in. He had an opened bottle of beer in one hand. Standing at the foot of the bed, he drank most of the beer then came round to stand over Gaunt. Wordlessly, he raised the bottle and let the rest of it splash down on Gaunt's face.

"You're a bastard," said Gaunt unemotionally.

Leiber laughed, took a farewell tug at the cord round Gaunt's neck, and left again.

The afternoon dragged past. Now and again, Gaunt could hear a distant murmur of traffic. There was a machine in the factory across the lane which worked with a slow, steady beat he more felt than heard. Leiber still made his routine visits but seemed to have become bored. A glance was usually enough, then he left.

Dusk closed in. The machine in the factory stopped and he saw a glow through the window which might be a street lamp.

He dozed off. When he wakened, it was dark outside the window but a light was on in the other room. He could hear voices. Leiber came in, accompanied by the fat-faced man who'd driven the Mercedes that morning.

"You're moving," said Leiber.

They freed his feet and removed the noose from his neck, then dragged him upright. When he tried to stand, his feet gave way under him.

Cursing, the two men half-carried, half-shoved him out of the room. From there he was pushed down the stairs and forced out into the yard, where the Mercedes was waiting, a white blob in the night. But he was swung round and pushed through another door, into the building's ground-floor workshop.

"What now?" asked Gaunt, as a light was switched on.

He looked around. The workshop area was half-filled with old packing-cases, and the few benches were grimy and cobwebbed, as if they hadn't been used in years.

"Over there." Leiber pointed at the nearest of the packing-cases. "Down beside it."

"Why?" asked Gaunt.

The two men exchanged a glance. Leiber shrugged.

"We're leaving you behind," he said.

"Dead or alive?"

As Gaunt spoke, the fat-faced man moved in to grab him. He dodged, still too unsteady on his feet to kick, and managed to use his head to butt the man on the face. He heard a howl of pain at the impact.

Then Leiber's revolver barrel chopped him across the skull and Gaunt went down, dazed and unable to move. The fat-faced man spat blood from his mouth, cursed, and helped Leiber drag Gaunt over to the packing-cases. Leiber produced two grubby yellow dusters from his pocket, forced one into Gaunt's mouth, then used the other to complete the gag. They tied his ankles again, pulling them up under him and taking a final turn of cord between his wrists and his feet.

"*Gasolina,*" said Leiber, standing back.

The other man went out. When he came back he was carrying a five-litre fuel can. Leiber took it from him with his left hand, still holding the revolver in his right. Then he put down the can, took a silencer from his pocket, and carefully screwed it onto the revolver's barrel.

"Mr. Garr sent a note." Leiber considered Gaunt calmly. "We don't need you any more." Pausing, he checked the silencer. "That's how it is."

Tight-lipped, Gaunt watched him take a half-step back. The gun came up. The fat-faced driver was grinning. Leiber suddenly swung the revolver and shot him between the eyes. The flat pop of the silencer blended with the thud as the other man hit the workshop floor, dead.

"Mr. Garr also said to keep down costs," said Leiber almost apologetically. "No outsiders."

Leiber took the car keys from the dead man's pocket. After laying down the revolver, he unscrewed the cap of the fuel can and allowed a little of the gasoline to slop out. Then he carried the can a short distance and laid it against the largest of the packing-cases. Taking out cigarettes and a book of matches, he lit a cigarette, drew on it carefully a couple of times until the tip glowed red, and tucked it into the matches. He placed the result on the floor close to the can, then picked up his gun.

"Mr. Garr said goodbye," he said, turning, and walked out.

For a moment, Gaunt stared at the glowing cigarette. It would take a minute or so, maybe more, to burn down like a fuse and ignite the matches. When that happened, he knew the rest. The heat would ignite the fuel can, turn it into an instant fire-bomb. The workshop would burn like tinder around him.

He tried to roll over, to get nearer, but he'd been tied too cleverly. In the dim light from the single overhead electric bulb, the face of the dead man on the floor still seemed to be grinning, mocking him.

Outside, the Mercedes started up. A brief glare of headlights reached the workshop as it turned and drove away.

Twisting and squirming, Gaunt managed a little way forward across the grimy concrete. Then again. He had achieved only a fraction of the distance by the time the cigarette had burned down enough for the red glow of its tip to be hidden behind the bookmatches.

There was a fizzing noise. Gaunt hunched his shoulders, trying to shelter his face as the matches flared. A split second later the fuel can exploded. The flat blast and shock wave of heat were followed by a yellow gout of flame. The nearest packing-cases began blazing, dried wood crackling and smoking as the fire spread with frightening rapidity.

Heat swept over him in waves. Sparks flew, widening the fire's grip. Then he heard noises he couldn't understand, noises which became a voice, shouting his name. Choking on the gag, he banged his heels on the concrete and kept doing it.

Coughing through the thickening smoke, two figures reached him and, as the flames licked nearer, hands seized him by the shoulders. He was dragged unceremoniously over the concrete in a rush that didn't stop until he was outside in the open, almost in the middle of the yard.

The gag was ripped from his mouth. Someone was using a knife to cut the cord at his wrists and ankles, and Carol Marek was crouching over him, repeating his name, her face white and strained in the yellow glow coming from the building.

"I'm okay." He managed to twist a bewildered grin. "Let me—let me get used to it."

"There was another man." She moistened her lips and glanced at the burning workshop. "What about him?"

"He's dead." Gaunt struggled up on his elbows then stared. There were others with her, all faces he recognized. He'd been rescued by some of Janos Barta's students. The nearest was carrying a pistol and smiled at him. It was Walter, the fair-haired young driver. A thought struck him. "We'd better get out of here."

She nodded and spoke rapidly to the rest of the group. Hauled to his feet, Gaunt cried out as cramp struck again, but strong young arms helped him stagger out of the yard and down the lane to the street at the far end.

Janos Barta's taxi was parked nearby. While Walter got behind the wheel, Carol helped Gaunt into the back seat then got in beside him. The other youngsters jumped into an old van waiting a short distance away.

The taxi began moving, the van starting up and following. Gaunt glanced back through the rear window. The first flames had begun to appear at the windows on the upper floor of the workshop building. Sighing, he slumped back against the cushions and closed his eyes.

When he opened them again, the taxi was being driven at a sedate pace along another street. Carol was sitting close, watching him anxiously.

"Thanks," he said fervently.

"Don't thank me." She indicated Walter, who was humming to himself as he drove. "They did it all."

"How?"

"Wait." She gripped his hand as a police car rushed towards them. It went past, heading in the opposite direction, siren wailing. Moments later, it was followed by a fire-engine. As both vanished down the road, she relaxed again. "Do you want to go to the hotel?"

"No." Gaunt shook his head. "Ask him to keep driving around for a spell." He waited until she'd spoken to Walter then said again, "How? Tell me how you got there."

"Walter and his friends are stubborn," Carol told him thankfully. "They didn't pay much attention when you said you didn't want them involved."

He blinked. "They were following me?"

"No, but they were keeping an eye on things." She shrugged and shook her head in admiration. "They heard you'd been arrested. They were watching when you were released but weren't near enough to do anything when Garr's men grabbed you. Then things got worse—they tried to follow the car and lost it. That's when Walter got in touch with me."

"I see." He chewed his lip. "How about Colonel Brozman? Did you tell him anything?"

Carol shook her head. "I nearly did, more than once. But all he knows is you haven't been seen since you were released. That was because of John Alford. He heard you'd been arrested—just about everyone in the hotel knew—and he began raising hell about it."

"He would." Gaunt grimaced at the thought. Alford had probably loved the chance to stir things up. "And Maggie Dimond?"

"She knew it looked as though Garr's men had you—I told her." Carol's grip on his hand tightened again. "But I'm more interested in you. Back there—"

"Garr doesn't want complications," he said dryly. "He decided he didn't need me any more." He saw her face and grinned encouragingly. "Look, I've a few dents—nothing more. But I want to know about Maggie Dimond. It matters."

"Still?" Her mouth tightened. "She wanted me to wait, do nothing. She seemed worried about you, yes, but she said she knew you wouldn't talk, that she believed Garr would probably only try to use you for some kind of deal. Then, after tonight—"

"Yes." Gaunt nodded. He saw Walter glance round at them. Leaning forward, he laid a hand on his shoulder and nodded again. Walter smiled cheerfully then concentrated on his driving. "Where is she now?"

Carol shook her head. "I don't know. She was in the hotel late this afternoon. After that, she disappeared. Brozman came looking for her later but went away. Then some of Walter's friends finally spotted the Mercedes and trailed it to that place. He got me, we came over, and"—her voice faltered at the memory—"we waited. The car drove off, we heard the explosion—"

"And saved me from frying." He sat silent for a moment, watching the traffic, a decision forming in his mind, the only one that was left. "Wherever Maggie Dimond is, she's with Valachova. But the rest fits—Garr must have managed to follow her this time. Now he's waiting to see what they'll do."

"Then you should let them get on with it," suggested Carol bitterly.

"No." He knew what he had to do. There was a risk, but at worst it was still acceptable—and he owed that much, at least, to Janos Barta and Barta's young followers. He glanced at his watch. It was almost 9 P.M. When he looked through the taxi's rear window, the old van was still trailing patiently. "Ask Walter to get rid of his friends, tell him I want to borrow that gun he's carrying and that I need his wheels just a little longer."

Carol Marek looked ready to protest for a moment. Then she sighed and nodded. She leaned forward and began talking.

The Skoda pulled in. Gloomily Walter drew his pistol from inside his jacket, handed it over, and got out and walked back to the van, which had stopped behind them. The pistol was an ancient

Mauser automatic, so old that Gaunt wondered who'd be in most danger if it was fired. He tucked it away then turned to Carol.

"I'm bringing Brozman into it."

"But—" Her eyes widened in surprise.

"Not the way you're thinking." He gave her a slight grin. "I need his help, and I believe I can get it."

"How?"

"First of all, he's got to be where I hope he is. Then I want you to make a phone call for me. Just a message, that Maggie Dimond has to see him urgently at the Smetana—and after that I've got to be on my own." He met her gaze firmly. "Totally, Carol—it has to be that way."

"And if it goes wrong?" she demanded.

"Then that's where it ends. I give up."

She looked relieved. Gaunt wondered how she would react if she knew what he really had in mind.

Walter returned after a couple of minutes. The van was already driving away as he got back behind the wheel of the Skoda.

From there, as they asked, he took them to Vaclav Square then down the little street past the night-club where Brozman had been their host. The grey Porsche was parked half-way along. Taking the next turn, the Skoda headed back to Vaclav Square and stopped at a public pay-phone booth.

Gaunt stayed in the taxi, watching, while Carol got out and used the telephone. She spoke briefly then hung up and came back.

"They'll tell him," she nodded.

"Good." Gaunt signalled to Walter and the taxi began moving again. He smiled at her. "Don't look so worried. I know what I'm doing."

"I hope so." Unexpectedly, she kissed him.

The taxi went down the same little street again. Gaunt left it just past Brozman's Porsche. As the taxi pulled away, he stepped into the shadow of a doorway and drew out the old Mauser pistol.

Barely a minute passed, then he heard footsteps. Anatole Brozman reached his car, keys in hand, and went towards the driver's door.

"Brozman." Gaunt stepped out, the Mauser trained on him. "Keep your hands where I can see them. Use the passenger side—but you're driving."

Brozman stiffened, stared at him, then slowly obeyed. His face was an impassive mask as he opened the passenger door, got in, and eased over behind the wheel. Gaunt followed him in, the Mauser still ready, and closed the door.

"Start driving. Keep it normal."

"You're mad," said Brozman.

The Porsche murmured to life and pulled away.

"Anywhere special?" asked Brozman.

"Not yet." Gaunt kept the pistol trained. "How was the funeral?"

Brozman's mouth tightened. He didn't reply.

"You said you wanted the people who killed him," said Gaunt. "You meant that?"

"Of course." Brozman gave him a flickering, sideways glance. "Why?"

"I want them too, for the same kind of reason." Gaunt drew a deep breath. "I think I can take you to them. But there are conditions."

Brozman swore under his breath. "What kind?"

"Your business is security. This isn't. If you get the men you want, anyone else around goes free." Gaunt paused. "You said the captain was your friend."

"He was." Brozman scowled at the road ahead. "These other people?"

"Haven't hurt anyone. You forget they exist—and we do the rest alone, you and I."

Brozman took a moment before he answered. "And if I say yes?"

"Then I've got to trust you, you've got to trust me," answered Gaunt.

"Interesting," murmured Brozman. He shrugged. "We can try."

"Good." Gaunt relaxed with a sigh. "Pull in." He waited until Brozman had brought the Porsche to a halt at the side of the road then, deliberately, he tossed the Mauser into the man's lap. "Does that help?"

"Yes." Carefully Brozman lifted the pistol. He frowned, gave a grunt of amusement. "Did this come from a museum?"

"I wouldn't know." Gaunt took out his cigarettes and lit one. He had three left. "Do we still have a deal?"

Brozman looked at the pistol, sighed, and nodded.

"Here's the story."

Gaunt kept it as simple as he could, edited out some areas like Janos Barta and the story of the plates, and watched Brozman's face while he talked. But Brozman hadn't got to be a colonel in Czech security through wearing emotions on his sleeve. Only once or twice did he show a flicker of surprise. He allowed himself a grunt of sheer incredulity when Gaunt first mentioned the Stuart link and the Sobieska jewels but stayed silent after that.

"What started this so-called treasure-hunt?" he asked at last. "If they've already found this silver, as they claim, that's one thing. But these Polish jewels—"

"Stopped being Polish a long time ago," murmured Gaunt. "It all began with Maggie Dimond doing some research."

"Then I suppose she conveniently found a map?" suggested Brozman.

"No, but Valachova did," said Gaunt. "Two maps. The first led them to the silver, like I told you—"

"And I have to believe all this, accept it." Brozman rubbed a hand along the steering wheel, as if appreciating its reality. "This—while we were waiting for something else."

"Like what?"

"Something you shouldn't be told," said Brozman slowly. "But maybe you have to know. We had a keen interest in people coming from Britain to the Trade Fair. We had reliable information that one of them would be a British intelligence agent, a courier of some kind. At first, I wondered a little about you." He shrugged. "We still don't know if one came. Perhaps the information was wrong. That happens."

"But it's why you had someone on the flight, why you were interested in the Smetana?"

Brozman nodded. "Officially, nothing else. My interest in Mrs. Dimond was—well, more personal. Now—" He gave a wry smile. "Yes, she is an unusual woman. But you've left something out. Your own motive, Mr. Gaunt."

"That's right. It stays that way."

"I see." Brozman raised the Mauser and, for a moment, pointed it at Gaunt. Then he nodded and tossed it back. "I have a few men I could trust implicitly. It wouldn't take long to get them."

"You and I," reminded Gaunt. "That was the deal."

"Yes." Suddenly Brozman laughed aloud. "And both of us crazy. Where do we go?"

When Gaunt told him, he knew the road and the Russian transport camp. He frowned for a moment.

"If this man Garr is following Mrs. Dimond and this Valachova, then he will probably let them do the work of finding the jewels before he does anything. He will make his move when they return to their vehicle. But I think I know another side-road near there. If we used that—" He stopped short.

Two uniformed militiamen were walking towards the Porsche, coming round to the driver's window. They moved casually, their rifles still slung from their shoulders. Gaunt looked at Brozman, then, as Brozman made a quick gesture, tucked the Mauser out of sight.

"Trust and trust," murmured Brozman.

He wound down the window. The pass he showed brought a ramrod stiffening from both militiamen. They saluted and moved on.

"Thanks," said Gaunt.

Brozman shrugged. He turned and faced Gaunt. "Understand one thing, Mr. Gaunt," he said. "In my job, I am a loyal professional. Tomorrow, I will be a loyal professional again. But, as you said, I was at a funeral today."

He started the Porsche. This time, the engine snarled as Brozman kicked the accelerator. It got under way with a squeal of rubber.

The Porsche was fast, Brozman handled it like an expert, and he drove with no particular regard for speed limits. In much less time than Gaunt had thought possible they had left the city behind and were on their way.

It was a strange alliance. Both knew it, both accepted it by a tacit avoidance of real conversation. Brozman admitted he had been in Britain once. He'd seen London, he'd watched the Changing of the Guard at Buckingham Palace, and he'd visited Karl Marx's grave at Highgate. Where else he'd been on that trip, what else he'd done, he kept to himself.

Gaunt found himself talking about other cities he'd visited and places he'd seen. It was as if, for both, there was a need to stay away from the real thoughts each had in his mind.

The Porsche ate the distance along the through highway, swung off onto the start of the network of country roads, and raced on through the night. Brozman was silent for a spell, concentrating on the twisting, narrow route. Suddenly he gave a strange laugh.

"I was thinking," he said, "if this goes well, it will be difficult to explain. If it goes wrong—"

"Then we've both got problems," agreed Gaunt.

A few kilometres more, and Brozman eased back on the accelerator. At last he gave a pleased grunt and changed down a gear. The Porsche murmured into a farm lane, swayed and bounced along its rough surface for another couple of minutes, then slithered to a halt. Brozman switched off lights and engine and signalled Gaunt out.

The sky overhead was cloudy but there was some moonlight. As Gaunt looked around at the silent, apparently empty fields on both sides of the track, Brozman opened the Porsche's front trunk lid. He brought out a compact machine-pistol, then considered Gaunt for a moment.

"For both our sakes, you need something better than that antique of a pistol," he mused. "Yes. Here—"

Gaunt caught the pump-action shotgun heaved in his direction.

"American," explained Brozman. "They make the best. Solid shot loaded—you know how to use it?" He grinned without humour in the moonlight as Gaunt nodded. "Then I'll lead."

They set off across the fields. After trudging a few minutes, they reached a hedge and Brozman, after hesitating, signalled they should follow its line. It ended at a junction with another hedge which flanked a narrow road.

"This is the one," murmured Brozman. He nodded to the left. "We follow it down. Quietly."

They came across the white Mercedes first. It was hidden just off the road, on a muddy track, and it was empty. But the radiator was still warm. Keeping to the field side of the hedge, they moved on again.

A light showed for a moment, not far ahead, then it went out. They froze, straining their eyes against the night. Gaunt tapped Brozman's shoulder and pointed. He could just make out the silhouette of a small van, parked beside some bushes.

The same light showed again and went out. Someone had used a torch close beside the van.

"Getting impatient," said Gaunt softly. "Tired of waiting." He shook his head as Brozman hefted the machine-pistol. "We need to be sure."

Brozman sighed and nodded. This time he let Gaunt lead as they went forward at a crouch, close under the shelter of the hedge. When they stopped, they were only a long stone's throw from the van. One man was there, squatting beside the front wheels. Suddenly, giving a soft grunt, Brozman pointed to the right. A second figure showed briefly, shifting position further along the hedge.

"You said three," hissed Brozman. "You're positive?"

Gaunt nodded, tight-lipped. Wherever the third man was located, he couldn't spot him. Until they knew, they couldn't move.

"They wait, we wait," muttered Brozman angrily. "All right. But you know what you're risking?"

He did, only too well. Maggie Dimond and Valachova had to be down at the old shrine, digging and hoping. Until they came back, whatever they achieved, nothing could be done. It meant using them, doing it coldly and deliberately, and praying that nothing went wrong.

Twenty minutes passed. The night was cold, the light wind rustled the leaves along the hedge, and the moon came and went as the clouds drifted overhead. Suddenly, Brozman nudged him hard.

Two figures were coming across the field, walking slowly, carrying something between them. He heard the soft click as Brozman checked the machine-pistol's safety-catch.

The two figures came nearer, until they were almost up to the van. Then another figure sprang to his feet a little way out in the open—the third man Gaunt and Brozman had been waiting on. Simultaneously, Matthew Garr's high-pitched voice called out.

It happened very fast.

The two figures with the box came to a startled halt. The one on the left reacted first, dropping his end of the box, pushing his companion aside. It was Stepan Valachova. He gave Maggie Dimond another shove, which sent her sprawling, and grabbed at his pocket.

As he dragged out the Luger he'd stolen from Gaunt, the men by the van fired first. Valachova jerked upright, staggered, then pitched forward—and the machine-pistol in Brozman's hands began a staccato, calico-ripping rasp which caught both gunmen in its hosing fury.

That left the third man. He fired two shots, the bullets zipping through the hedge close to Brozman. Bringing up the pump-action shotgun, Gaunt sighted and triggered in one smooth movement.

And it was over.

Maggie Dimond struggled to her feet, unhurt. She stared almost blindly towards Gaunt and Brozman then went down on her knees beside Valachova. As she touched him, he gave a faint moan.

Brozman turned away, padding off to check the man lying further out. Quietly, Gaunt went over and joined Maggie Dimond. In the moonlight, he could see the two bullet wounds in Stepan Valachova's chest and the blood frothing on his lips every time he drew breath.

"You." Valachova saw him and forced a grin. "I—I was right, eh? We found our box."

Gaunt glanced at Maggie Dimond. Somehow she forced a smile for Valachova's benefit.

"You found it," said Gaunt softly. "And we got Garr."

"Good." Valachova's eyes misted with pain for a moment. "I—we dug where I thought. It was there. Now open it—tell me."

"Maggie." Gaunt touched her arm. She shook her head and he went alone to where the small, earth-stained chest was lying. Framed by metal bands, it was fastened at the lid by a hasp which was solid with rust.

Brozman came out of the night to join him and frowned at the chest.

"This is it?"

Gaunt nodded, then looked past him. "What about them?"

"Dead." Brozman's voice was flat and unemotional. "All three. The one you shot was Garr—at least that's what it says on his passport." He pursed his lips. "You knew it had to be this way? Otherwise—"

"I knew," said Gaunt deliberately.

He lifted the shotgun and brought the butt down sharply on the hasp of the chest. The rusted metal disintegrated under the blow.

Brozman had a torch. He switched it on and played the beam on the chest as Gaunt forced the lid. Then he gave a startled grunt, squatted down, looked again, and gave another grunt which became a cynical chuckle.

"You call this a king's treasure?" he asked.

All that was in the chest was a plate. Its edges showed through the mildewed cloth in which it had been wrapped. Silently, Gaunt parted more of the cloth and looked at the pattern of lines and blotches across its face.

"Someone else got here first, a long time ago."

Brozman grinned at him. "A joker as well as a thief, eh? He takes a fortune and leaves an old kitchen plate for some future fool."

"It looks that way," said Gaunt.

"It does," said Maggie Dimond in a flat, dull voice. She was standing behind them and turned to Gaunt. "He wants you." She moistened her lips. "He hasn't got long."

He left her with Brozman and hurried over to kneel beside Valachova. The man's eyes, bright and eager, met his own.

"You've seen?" asked Valachova in a hoarse, forced whisper.

"Yes." Gaunt nodded and lied. "You were right. The jewels are there."

"No." Valachova tried to shake his head. His blood-flecked lips shaped a smile. "I—I carried that chest. It was too light, not heavy enough. But at least I found it, eh?" He moved a hand feebly, beckoning Gaunt closer. "Do something for me. In my inside pocket —an envelope."

Gaunt reached in, found the envelope, and brought it out.

"There is an address inside. Go there, say I—I sent you, and they have a parcel. It is the money I got from Garr, for the silver." Valachova's breathing was a shallow rasp as he fought to go on. "Your friend who died—you said there were others like him. Give it to them. Ideals need money to stay alive. Or at least—at least money helps."

"It helps," agreed Gaunt.

Valachova sighed, started to smile again, then went limp. The rasping breathing faded and stopped.

Brozman was coming over. Before he arrived, Gaunt slipped the envelope in his pocket.

"Dead?" asked Brozman.

Gaunt nodded.

"A pity." Brozman scowled absently. "But again it makes things easier." He thumbed across the fields. There were headlights approaching. "My Russian friends have decided to see what the shooting was about."

The headlamps were moving fast. "What will you tell them?"

"That I'm a colonel in Czech counter-intelligence, with some good KGB connections." Brozman squared his shoulders grimly. "That should quieten them. After that, I have a reasonable imagination. But I still have a problem—two problems to be precise."

Gaunt looked across to where Maggie Dimond was standing. "Us?"

Brozman nodded. "I'll get you back to Prague. Tomorrow you'll both be on the first flight out to the West—wherever it's going. Regrettably, neither of you will be welcome in this country again." He paused. "Still, maybe you should have a souvenir."

Gaunt stared as Brozman held out the plate from the chest. "That?"

Brozman shrugged. "She doesn't want it. I asked. So—"

"I'll take it." Gaunt took the plate from him. "About tomorrow—"

"Tomorrow you will be on that plane." Brozman frowned. "Now, make sure everything looks right before we have company."

Two days later Jonathan Gaunt was back in Edinburgh, sitting in Henry Falconer's office while the old grandfather clock ticked solemnly in its corner and the senior administrative assistant read slowly through his report for the second time.

He thought back as he waited.

The Russian troops, a somewhat apprehensive squad led by a half-dressed sergeant, had been dealt with by Brozman in crushing style. But it had still been late before they'd got back to Prague, even later before Gaunt had been able to snatch a few hours sleep.

At 7 A.M. two of Brozman's men had been there to collect him and take him to the airport with Maggie Dimond. They'd been put on the first aircraft out, a Lufthansa flight for Munich.

Gaunt smiled to himself. Carol had Valachova's envelope and would get it to Janos Barta's former students. When she flew home at the end of the week, he'd be at the airport. Maggie Dimond had flown on with him to London, where she had decided to stay for a while. If she wanted, she could probably slide back into her Inland Revenue routine, but it was doubtful if she would.

Falconer cleared his throat and glanced up.

"It—ah—was different from what I expected," he said carefully. His broad face showed a mixture of emotions for a moment. "If I'd known—"

"You didn't," reminded Gaunt.

"No." Falconer seemed to struggle with himself then to reach a decision. "I've a small confession to make. This—well, suggestion by Colonel Brozman that there might have been a British intelligence agent on your flight out—"

"What about it?" Gaunt saw Falconer's expression and leaned forward. "Henry, if you're trying to tell me something, get on with it."

"There was an Intelligence aspect," said Falconer uneasily. "Did you meet a man called John Alford?"

"Him?" Gaunt said it incredulously.

"His wife," said Falconer. "I'm told she's a damned good courier. Alford's business is genuine but he also covers for her. I gather she's —well, not the type you'd expect."

"No." Gaunt thought of the fat, dowdy woman and marvelled for a moment. "You knew about it?"

Falconer nodded. "Her—ah—superiors told us. They liked the idea of you being out at the same time, hoped you might confuse things a little for the opposition."

"Nice of them," said Gaunt sarcastically. "I suppose I did."

"Yes." Falconer cleared his throat hastily. "Just one thing. The plate Brozman gave you. You brought it back?"

"It got broken," said Gaunt neutrally. "An accident—I didn't think you'd want the bits."

"No." Falconer returned to the report again.

Gaunt mentally apologized for the lie. But it had seemed better that way. On the Lufthansa flight out of Prague he'd borrowed a carafe of water from one of the stewardesses.

Charles Edward Stuart or whoever else had buried the chest behind the old shrine hadn't been playing any kind of joke. Instead, they'd been acting very carefully. The plate was another map, one even Gaunt could recognize.

He still wasn't sure why he'd deliberately broken the plate. But would the Queen's and Lord Treasurer's Remembrancer or anyone else had thanked him for bringing it back if they'd seen what it showed?

Westminster Abbey constituted one hell of an area to start searching for a mythical treasure. And the paint on the plate had flaked just enough with age to make it impossible to know exactly where to look.

The Sobieska jewels might as well stay undisturbed. Perhaps it was right they should.

"You're due some time off," said Falconer, looking up. "Made any plans?"

"A few," agreed Gaunt.

"And—ah—any thoughts about a car again?" queried Falconer mildly.

Gaunt shook his head. Not before the end of the month, and his next pay-cheque.

He wondered if he should telephone Patti and congratulate her on her news. Maybe he would, maybe he wouldn't.

He could ask Carol what she thought.

NOTE:

The Sobieska jewels existed—and many of them vanished. Charles Edward Stuart wandered Europe for many years after the '45 Rebellion and was widely believed to have at least one illegitimate son during that period.

One fact firmly documented is that a few years after he escaped from Scotland he made a secret visit to London. One reason was to sound out possible support from Jacobites. There may have been another.

Refraction paintings from that time still exist.

N.W.

Noah Webster is the pseudonym of a popular and prolific mystery writer who is known for the unusual locales of his novels. This is the seventh novel to feature Jonathan Gaunt, who was introduced to Crime Club readers in *Flickering Death*. Recent Jonathan Gaunt adventures include *An Incident in Iceland, A Pay-off in Switzerland,* and *A Witchdance in Bavaria.* The author lives in Scotland with his wife and three children.